BLADES OF DEATH!

The two thick-set samurai were naked to the waist. They drew their glistening swords and shouted a challenge.

Ted Rockson reached for his shotpistol only to find an empty holster. *Lost the damn thing somewhere!* There was only one recourse, the long, heavy Katama sword he carried. He pulled it from his scabbard.

The Doomsday Warrior was not an expert at swordplay. But Chen had taught him a few lessons in the noble art in Century City's gymnasium. Lessons that would be tested now, Rockson thought grimly, as the two samurai suddenly rushed forward swinging their razor-sharp blades over their heads like deadly twin scythes!

DOOMSDAY WARRIOR

#13 AMERICAN PARADISE

BY RYDER STACY

ZEBRA BOOKS
KENSINGTON PUBLISHING CORP.

FOREWORD

America was a strange and often frightening place one hundred and nine years after World War III. Radioactive deserts, killer dog packs and poisonous creeper vines now were the norm in a world gone mad.

The Red victors of the Nuke War were hard put to maintain their grip on the nation in such conditions. But to the Freefighters, led by a remarkable soldier of survival named Ted Rockson, this bizarre world was *home sweet home*. Rockson, known as the Doomsday Warrior, was the acknowledged leader of the battle against the Soviets.

Ted Rockson was six feet two, tan and musclar, and *hard*. His long, black hair with the mutant's white streak in the middle was thrown back over his shoulders. His mismatched aqua and ultramarine eyes were steady and keen. He was a born leader and a stubborn go-it-alone individual. And above all, he had a fierce hatred of tyrants.

Rock, as the Freefighters called him, carried a versatile balisong knife in his belt; there was a twelve-gauge shotpistol in his right holster, and a snub-nosed Liberator SMG slung over his arm.

Operating out of a hidden fortress city in the Rocky Mountains, Rockson led his Rock team on mission after mission against the enemy.

The team consisted of the cream of the crop of Century City's awesome fighters for freedom:

1) Detroit—a bull-necked, ebony man with a pitching arm that could strike out any inter-free-city home run hitter, or eliminate a Red bunker fortification. He carried twenty of his "pineapples" on crisscrossed bandoliers on his chest. Detroit was also an expert anthropologist—a necessary skill in a post-nuke America with a thousand bizarre, isolated cultures.

2) Chen—the pencil-moustached, wiry, Chinese-American martial arts expert. He carried a belt load of *shuriken,* star knives, for throwing. Chen often sparred with Rockson, the only man that could win so much as a draw against him. He hated formality and often wore a mocking grin when people spoke but said little himself.

3) Archer—an immense, black-bearded mountain man. Rockson had found him sinking in a quicksand pool while Rock was out on a mission. He saved the near-mute, and Archer had repaid him in kind many times. Archer preferred isolation to company. He lived deep in the twisting maze of conduits under Century City and was loathe to wear a khaki uniform like the others. Instead, he lived and slept in a bearskin outfit. You could overlook his smell, because Archer had a homemade titanium alloy bow

and a set of arrows that could pierce a six-inch armor plate.

4) Scheransky—a blond Soviet defector, the technical expert. He was the most recent addition to the team. Scheransky carried the standard Liberator, plus a Czar's bludgeon. He wore a pair of pearl-handled .44 revolvers—a gift from Dr. Schecter, Century City's chief scientist, for Scheransky's assistance to him.

5) McCaughlin—a bear of a man, nearly as bulky as Archer. But in all other ways he was the opposite. He had a neatly trimmed, reddish beard and a crisp uniform. He was talkative and gregarious, with a special penchant for the ladies. The crew-cut fighter was also a passable trail cook and a humorist. He was a must on all missions, for when the going got rough, McCaughlin's wit got going! Plus he was, like the others, a crack shot.

There was no stopping these determined men. With Rockson in the lead, surely AMERICA WOULD RISE AGAIN!

just left was under water. Down the dunes beyond it

CHAPTER 1

Fog. Endless fog. That was the way it had been for two days now, once the Rock team left the heights of the Sierra Nevada and descended to the barren valley of California. Rockson was hoping they would reach the coast soon. All the men — Archer, Scheransky, McCaughlin, Detroit and even Chen who was noted for his patience — were getting restless. Maybe restless wasn't the word. They were almost driven crazy now by the monotony, the silence. And the moisture was rotting everything: their clothing, packs, even their well-worn boots. This sullen evenness, this blindness, was worse on the nerves than the shaking and quaking of the "Unstable Lands" of Nevada, which had sent the men's sturdy 'brid mounts down into suddenly gaping crevasses, along with most of their ammunition. The six men survived to tramp on toward the Pacific waters. Six sullen, sodden men in moods so sour Rockson felt they didn't need any weapons, they would spit acid at anything that bothered them!

Most of all, he didn't like being in fog in unknown territory. In the Rockies there were dangers galore, but he knew the dangers. Here — who knew whether an innocent-looking bush had mutated into a grabbing thing that would yank you off your feet and digest you?

As he sloshed through inches-deep mud at the head of the column, barely able to see six feet ahead of him, Rockson thought back to how this expedition had begun: He had been deep in Century City's underground archives. Historical researchers had unearthed a video tape from the nuclear war, and though it was 109 years old, they managed to restore it. It was a recording by Shiela Martin—one of the underground city's founders. Rockson had placed the tape in an antique VCR and had been watching it for a half hour. Martin, on the tape, was reporting to the third council meeting regarding a drilling operation that had resulted in the second of the many levels of Century City being completed. Rock had been amazed to actually see and hear this woman of legend and was deeply absorbed. Then the annoying interruption came.

It was old man Rath, the hawk-nosed intelligence chief, who brought word of the faint, garbled radio broadcast from one of the most far-flung groups of Freefighters—the Surfcombers—in California. The message was something about a new weapon about to fall into Soviet hands. Rath made Rock turn off the precious tape and demanded that Rock "quit this foolishness" and secure that weapon. He produced a document ordering Rock to do so, a resolution by the council.

Now here he was, his hat brim dripping water in his face, Rock's expression set in a constant grimace,

10

battling fatigue and rot.

Rockson's left boot suddenly touched something gritty; he looked down and saw that there was sand under his feet. He called a halt to the column and stood still, listening to a low roar.

"What do you make of that?" asked the bull-necked, muscular black man, trying to peer through the dense fog.

"Detroit," Rock replied, "I — think it's the roar of *surf!*"

They walked forward slowly, inhaling pungent salt air as the fog parted. They *were* on a beach. Ahead was the Pacific Ocean, breakers and all.

McCaughlin came up alongside the Doomsday Warrior.

"Well I'll be, Rock. Are we at our destination?"

"Not sure . . ." Rock replied. "We're on the coast, obviously, but maybe too far north or south. Chen, take a reading on the geo-locator."

Now that the sun shone palely through the clouds, the mini-sextant-gyrocompass device could be set down on its tripod in the sand to determine their position. That was exactly what the martial-arts expert proceeded to do. When he threw the switch, there were a few beeps, and a red readout appeared on the globular six-inch device.

"We're twelve miles too far north — not bad," Chen reported.

"Well, let's get trekking then," their leader said.

Chen scooped up the geo-locator, snapped its tripod shut and put it back in his rucksack. The weary men, buoyed by being so near their goal, walked down the beach with a bit of their old spirit.

After a while, Rock looked back. One man was missing. "Hold it," he ordered. "Let's go back, Archer's disappeared."

They found him way down the beach, bending over."

"*Archer,* stop picking up seashells," Rock admonished. "We can't carry those around!"

"Pretty!" the giant replied sheepishly. "Meee liike!"

"Oh, all right, but just the small ones."

Rockson smiled, remembering when he first had laid eyes on the near-mute mountain man. He had dragged Archer from a quicksand pit, and that was the beginning of a long and beautiful friendship. The mountain man's home-made steel arrows were a good complement to the other men's special abilities. Archer had gotten them out of many scrapes with his mighty bow, but the man was . . . unpredictable.

Speaking of scrapes, Rock thought. He was feeling a prickle on the back of his neck. His mutant senses were picking up danger.

"Archer, drop those things, and keep your arrows ready. Men, get on full alert!"

"Is something up?" asked Scheransky, the blond was cross-drawing his new silver .44s from his pair of embossed leather holsters.

"Maybe . . . maybe not."

They listened for a while. Nothing but the wind and surf and an eerie silence beyond. No bird noises — nothing.

Rock finally said, "Must be a false alarm—let's get moving.

Still, as they walked in the slate-colored light, Rock could feel the electricity in the air.

A sound—a noise like the muttering of mad children—arose from the fog. The sound coalesced into shouts of at least a dozen men. Indescipherable, but angry.

"Get down!" Rock yelled, taking out the fog-piercing infrared binocs as he hit the sand. He trained them down the beach toward the ruckus. But he didn't need the lenses!

They were right on the Freefighters now, six snarling, drooling cavemen, spinning bola-like weapons overhead, which they proceeded to throw. Most of the swirling rope-and-rocks missed. But Archer, who was slow to hit the sand, got entangled in the sticky weblike things. Then, as the Freefighters raised their weapons, they were pounced on by the huge animal-skin-clad, red-eyed attackers.

A knife flashed down at Rock, but the caveman's blade never met the mark. The beast-man who pounced on the Doomsday Warrior was met by sixteen explosive pellets of his shotpistol. He flew back from Rockson, the burning X-pattern of holes in the thing's chest trailing smoke.

Rockson sat up and spun the pistol toward Archer who, trussed in a caveman's ropes, was having a hard time fending off his attacker. Once again Rock fired, careful to aim wide. Half the pattern of explosive pellets impacted on the caveman. He fell away from Archer, his face like raw hamburger.

Archer snapped the ropes and pulled his shotpistol, taking down one more. Very quickly, the primitives were shot stone-dead. The only Freefighter injury was a knife cut on Detroit's left upper arm.

But the battle wasn't over. A second group, ten immense fur-clad prehistoric men, was down the beach, just watching. Perhaps they had meant to join the attack but now were wary. Their eyes glinted grey in the smeary light of the pale sun, looking like dead, cold rocks filled with only a vacuum, not any soul.

They crouched down and looked at one another, as if considering whether to attack or flee. Meanwhile, the embattled Freefighters clambered to their feet. The 8 foot tall man-creatures seemed to study the spilled bodies of their compatriots on the red-stained sands of the beach. Rockson expected them to retreat.

Instead, one of the primitives made a decision for the whole group. With a snarl he raced forward, raising his huge stone adze on high. His speed was staggering, and Rockson yelled, "Fire!" as he let a whole clip of "X" pellets blast from his shotpistol.

The other Freefighters also laid down a withering pattern of hot lead with their 9mm Liberators SMGs or their hand-held deathdealers. The cavemen-types were hit five, six, seven times each, and fell in crazy rag-doll fashion only a few feet away.

Then only silence. The wind. The breakers.

Was that it? Rock sure hoped so. Then Rockson sensed something—and whirled. Just in time.

The primitive attackers, it appeared, could be very

14

stealthy as well as fast. Some more of them had come around in the fog, outflanking the Freefighters. There were at least fifty of the bastards creeping from less than ten yards away. They had moved silently, as if they had cats' paws, not hairy human feet.

"By Lenin," whispered Scheransky. "How many of the suckers are there?"

"Don't waste talk, just shoot them," Rock ordered.

Again they laid down a pattern of intense fire. But this bunch had something new — flatstone shields! Even the armor-piercing bullets of the Freefighter's Liberator rifles pinged off crude but effective barriers.

"Oh-oh," Chen commented, "time for more than bullets!"

Rock picked up on Chen's suggestion, saying, "Shoot your arrows, Archer! Chen — use the explosive star darts! Detroit — hit 'em with the grenades!"

Archer had already pulled an arrow from his quiver and notched it into the steel bow's string. He fired the explosive-tipped arrow almost straight up. Rockson, for a second, feared the arrow would catch on the wind and fall right back on them. But it didn't. It impacted on the sand just behind the center of the advancing group of smelly beast-men and exploded with a sizeable concussion.

The metal shields collapsed forward from the blast, and those primitives that weren't taken down by the explosion, were blasted by the star darts and grenades which were now lobbed at the exposed attackers.

"Let 'em have it with the Liberators!" Rock commanded.

The remaining attackers rushed forward waving heavy stone mallets but fell like wheat before a scythe in the 9mm death-storm.

Again, silence, except for one fallen caveman, who twitched and groaned from time to time. The Doomsday Warrior thought it was over at last.

Then came the sound of more than a hundred garbled voices screaming something like "Vengeance — vengeance — *vengeance!*"

The sun had burned off more of the fog, and Rockson could faintly see the high, rolling dunes along this particular stretch of beach. And pouring over the dunes were hordes of monster-sized fur-clad attackers.

It didn't look good. Their ammo was nearly gone, and the army of cave people was running at them with axes and knives and bludgeons held on high, screaming bloody murder.

Now there was another noise, this time from out on the waves. More voices, but not jabbering. The new voices were shouting, "Doom for Invaders. Doom! *Doom!*"

Were the Freefighters being hit from sea as well as land?

The cavemen, hearing the voices from the sea, froze in position and sniffed the air. Rockson was puzzled. Who was coming from the sea — and how?

He still saw nothing but breakers.

Then, from out over the surf, a set of flaming golden tridents flashed overhead and into the cavemen's ranks. One struck off a leather-clad primitive's head and another golden trident solidly pierced through the chest of another attacker. The strange weapons fizzled, and Rock could smell burning skin.

The second caveman still stood, the glowing-hot trident buried in his chest. He staggered forward as his eyes rolled up. Blood came out of his nose and ears. He gurgled some startled words and lifted his crude ax to strike. But Rockson kicked his legs out from under him and delivered a coup-de-grace from his shotpistol.

As a dozen more golden tridents flew over the Rock team at the cavemen, the man-creatures turned and fled for their lives, abandoning their dead and wounded.

The unseen friends behind the breakers now came flashing forward on the whitecaps, riding silver surfboards toward the Freefighters at amazing speed. In all, there were seven muscular, bronze-skinned men on long tapered surfboards. A strange throwing device was still held up in one hand of each surfer while the other arm balanced the ride on the waves.

Rockson said, "Well I'll be! These guys must be the Surfcombers that sent the message for us to come see them—"

"Kriiiyah!" one bronze man yelled and hurled a trident straight at Rockson. He dove to the side, rolled and pointed his pistol seaward.

The Doomsday Warrior yelled, "Hey stop throwing—or we'll fire back! We come in peace. I'm Rockson, Ted Rockson. Hold your fire!"

Again the surfboard riders, sliding expertly back and forth on the breakers, let loose another set of flaming tridents. These the men were hard-put to avoid, and one nicked McCaughlin's left arm.

"Damn," Rock yelled. "Either they can't hear me over the roar of the waves, or they mean us harm! Better use the flare cartridges. Fire over their damned blond heads!"

The Freefighter squad switched to flare shells with the twist of a dial on the handle of the weapons. They fired nearly in unison—high. Their red flare shells burst out of the big-barrelled weapons and streaked up over the surf riders, exploding with percussive brilliance.

That put the fear of God into the surfers. They hit the water, spilling off their boards and tumbling in the surf.

Then, over the crashing surf, Rockson faintly heard, "Hold your fire, intruders. If you are not enemies—identify yourselves."

Rock shouted, "That's better," and lowered his weapon. "Keep your guard up, men," he said more softly. "I don't know who these characters are—"

The surfers retrieved their boards and paddled them in. Then they stood up, and the seven bronze men, carrying their boards, stepped forward through the waves. Every one of them was tracked by the keen eyes of the Freefighters.

The most muscular and blond man of the bunch emerged from the water. He put his board down on the sand as he came forward from the others. He was holding one of the odd tridents cradled in his arms. He looked, with his bronze skin and long blond locks tangled with seaweed, like some god-damned Neptune Agonistes.

"Who did you say you were?"

"I'm Ted Rockson—who the hell are you?"

The big blond man came closer. His surprising yellow eyes surveyed Rock carefully. Then he smiled a perfect white-toothed grin.

"Yeah, I suppose you *could* be Rockson—you have the white streak in your hair and those mis-matched blue eyes."

"I'm Rockson, alright. Put down your weapons, we come in peace. Now that you know who I am. Who are you?"

"We're the Surfcombers, man, you know—the ones who sent for you? I'm Chief Knudson, and this here," he said, turning and pointing, "is Manny, my assistant."

He motioned for a taller, thinner man with mirror sunglasses on to come over and stand next to him. Then he pointed at the other five men, who wore scant, sea-green swim trunks and nothing else, iden-tifying each in turn. "This is Damian Simley, and these other fellows are Alf and Billy and Tex, and last but not least, old Sammy. We're pleased to meet you, Rockson."

Chief Knudson extended his arm, and Rock started to take his hand; but the man slipped his hand past Rockson's and locked forearms. He shook Rock's forearm. "Pleased to meet a fellow American."

"And I'm pleased to meet you, Chief Knudson." Rock sighed. "I think I can say for all of us, thanks for helping out against those—hairy guys. But after helping us, why did you fire on us?"

"Mistaken identity. We have trouble along this beach. It's hard to keep our territory intact. Besides the Tragos—that's the group that attacked you—there are a lot of other primitive folk roaming around the dunes that try to take over this beach. We manage to keep our surf-turf though, since they're more primitively armed than we are. As for why we fired on you Freefighters—those khakis you're wearing are a lot like those worn by the group we call the Marauders. They come down here from time to time and steal our crab traps right out from under our noses. There's a mess of crab traps just yards from here."

"I see . . . that explains it. Now which if you is the man that reported the Soviets have acquired a secret weapon?"

The chief smiled. "Ah, that would be Murf Cross, our best explorer. He's back at the beach shack—our headquarters. You'll meet him."

"Good," said Rock. "As soon as possible." Then he introduced the Freefighters one by one. "This big fellow is Archer—he's a mountain man and a bit taciturn. The other big guy is McCaughlin. And then this friend is Chen." The pencil-moustached Chinese-American smiled mockingly as he always did at the formalities. "Then we have Detroit Green—our grenade man and team anthropologist.

And last but not least, our Russian friend, Scheransky."

"Scheransky?" the chief questioned.

"Yes," Rockson smirked. "Not all Russians are Reds, you know. He's our technical expert and a loyal Freefighter."

It was getting colder, and the sky started sprinkling down rain. Archer coughed and took off his hat and squeezed it dry. With his hat removed, one could see his crystal-impregnated scalp. Red and blue sparks occasionally flared in the crystals, attracting Knudson's comment.

"What the hell?" muttered the chief. "This Archer fellow has a most unusual topside!"

"It's a long story—a repair job after his head was split open in a fight. Archer, put your hat back on. The sparks will attract birds."

Archer nodded gravely. "Meee sorrry."

"Not too long on intellect, but a regular Robin Hood with his hand-made arrows," Rock said warmly. "And a walking light show when he takes his hat off."

"Well," said the Surfcomber chief, "let's get back to headquarters and out of the rain—ever eat barbequed steamers?"

Archer fairly drooled his way along the beach. They soon saw the long, low-slung beachcomber shack ahead. The wooden rambling structure had a thousand car hubcaps with familiar names from the past—Mitsubishi, Oldsmobile, Toyota—plastered on its weathered walls.

CHAPTER 2

The Freefighters and their guides had to bend to get in the low entrance of the ramshackle-appearing structure. But once they were inside, Rockson found the ceiling wasn't as low as he had expected, for they stepped *down* into a broad, seashell-adorned room. He realized that the exterior made the place look low and poorly constructed, but it wasn't. The driftwood and scrap outside was only surface dressing.

The room was about 50 feet square and lit by concealed electric bulbs behind decorative — and translucent — seashells, large ones. There were heavy, rough-hewn beams in the ceiling and five or six treclike, vertical support pillars scattered about. The walls, besides being full of shelves containing myriad technical and how-to manuals, were racked with weapons: guns, huge machetes, hook-and-grapples. Plus, there were rows of those golden tridents that had proven so effective.

This whole set-up called for a re-evaluation. Rock had thought initially that the Surfcombers were a low-tech group. How wrong he was. The more he

23

observed, including a gape out a rear window at the several dune buggies parked in the ramp, the more he understood they were very *high*-tech!

A swivel chair that had been facing the other way whirred, and the chief introduced its smiling, blond occupant, Murf Cross. Cross had been viewing a chair-arm-installed, tri-D video, which he now turned off. "Crazy man," he said rising, "glad to meet the famous Doomsday Warrior."

The man was an easy six feet five inches of long, muscular bronze. His armshake was powerful. Rockson accepted a beer and then sat down in another cool leatherette swivel chair that the chief brought for him. He leaned intensely toward the muscular Cross and got right to business. "What about this radio broadcast you sent to Rath at Century City? What is the weapon you spoke of that the Russians have? Did you *see* it?"

"It's real enough," Murf stated, "but I didn't see it. It was described to me. Here, take a look."

Murf fished down under his seat and produced a water-rumpled sketch pad. "Good thing I use waterproof ink when I draw, and not charcoal. Here, look at this sketch."

Rock opened the eight-by-eleven pad to the first page. The first drawing was of a nativelike house — broadbeamed, covered with carved wood faces. In front of the house, there was a set of most attractive, near-naked, island maidens. "No, a few pages on," Murf apologized.

Rock flipped through several more pages of sketched native girls.

Murf said, "Those drawings are my studies of the natives of Rarapani—that's where the crystal weapon was stolen from. Rarapani is eight thousand miles from here, in the middle of the Pacific Ocean. It was a paradise until the Reds came." Rockson had reached the last of twelve pages and had yet to see a picture of anything that looked like a weapon—or a crystal.

Murf said, "Not there? Oh wow! That's right. I left it in my room—I *think*." He grinned sheepishly. "Come on," he said, putting down his beer on the chair-arm video, "let's go to my room. The drawings I made of the crystal weapon—from native descriptions—must be in there."

He led Rock along seashell-and-netting-covered walls of a long corridor, explaining as they walked, "We each have our own pad, of course, even though the beach shack is one big building." He opened a rustic wood door and turned on a light inside since the room had no window.

Rockson entered behind the Surfcomber. He saw lots of driftwood that had been made into lamps, and even the bed was made of a wide log.

"Like it?" the crew-cut, blond surfer asked.

"Er—very—beachy," Rock said, noncommittaly.

There was a glossy photo of a bare-breasted Polynesian girl on the dresser. A girlfriend? Plus a set of tikis—faces carved of greenstone and worn on a necklace—hung on the wood-plank walls. Also there were fierce war god masks.

"All stuff from my trip," explained Murf. "I would have brought more back, if I could have. I didn't want to come back at all; I liked it there in Rarapani. You can see why." He pointed at the girl's photo. "That's Mirani — she's neat!"

"Where are the sketches of the weapon," Rock insisted impatiently.

"Oh, sorry, here." He picked up a sketch pad off the dresser and handed it to Rockson.

Rock again flipped through sketches, this time of fierce-looking male Polynesians standing next to outrigger canoes on a pristine white-sand beach amid fronds of palms.

"I still don't see any weapon!" Rock was getting very frustrated. And he didn't like Murf's flippant manner.

Interrupting his words, a blond girl in a scant leather bikini came in with a tray of beers. She was nearly as tall as Murf and very buxom. She smiled gently, set down the two foamy glasses and left. She was the first Surfcomber woman Rock had seen.

"Our women are modest and stay in the B.G." said the beachboy. "The way women should."

Rock made no comment. Each U.S. subculture had its own customs.

"Surf's up!" Murf said, chugging the beer. "We have our own brewery, you know." He burped, then popped open another can.

Rock didn't touch his beer. Was this a wild-goose chase? He fumed, "Where the hell is the weapon drawing?"

"Oh *damn* it. I remember now! I left the pad with the drawing of the crystal weapon in the beach buggy. I'm *sure* it's there." Murf slapped his head with his right palm.

Rockson sat down heavily on the surfboard-shaped cot. Was there a weapon? Was this handsome surfer just a flake? But he controlled his anger. Maybe he's forgetful or drunk. Or *maybe* he's testing me, seeing if I get angry. These people were very different from the Freefighters. They were a long-isolated race of Americans. Their casual, forgetful ways sure didn't stop them from developing a high-tech radio, those power tridents and a whole lot of other gadgets. He'd just have to remain calm and cool. Cultures are very different, and sometimes you have to be patient when first meeting them!

Still, it was with exasperation that Rock said, "I sure hope there are drawings of a weapon in the buggy."

"Don't worry, I have them. Relax. We'll go get them now. But get a little more laid back, man. After all, *life is a beach*."

Rock smiled. "Okay. No particular hurry, *man*. I'll go — when you're ready."

Murf said, "Hey then, come on, I'm not an overly organized person you know. That organization-bag is the old bag that got America and the world in big trouble once. God, all that *rushing* around. We Surfcombers are more — how do you say it? Cooled out! Out here on the beach, time is NOTHING! But, I'll show you the picture and tell you all I remember about what the Rarapanians said about the crystal. Let's just finish the beers that Sandy brought us. Then I swear by my jockstrap that you'll see the sketches!"

Rock slowly drank several of the cold beers, while silently looking around the room, trying to get "laid back."

Finally, Murf burped and said, "Well, maybe *now* you'll ride with me down the beach a ways in my dune buggy. I'm in charge of setting up a clambake for the sunset club—that's all of us. It's pretty watching the sun set when the fog isn't so thick. You can look at the sketch while I set up the party."

Rock nodded. "Sure, no hurry." Every race and sub-race he had visited in America, all isolated groups of survivors of the "big war" as they usually called it, had developed their own *infuriating* culture. If this one was laid back he'd have to adjust to it!

They left the room and walked out a door and across a sandy ramp. Rockson wondered if the other men, who had stayed in the big meeting room, were now half as drunk as he was. Those home-brew beers sure were *strong*.

They were out behind the shack on the sandy rear ramp. Murf went to one of the ten, huge-wheeled, dune buggies, stopped at one with tiger-stripe paint and climbed up into one of the two bucket seats.

"Hop up, man."

Rock did, noting the big vehicle had a heavy rollbar. God, he thought, how often do these things turn over?

He did as Murf instructed—strapped himself into the hard bucket seat next to the blond driver. The eager beachboy turned a switch, and Rockson heard the big diesel engine turn over and catch.

"There's four hundred horses under the hood," Murf bragged, "so hold on to your hat."

They roared up the ramp at breakneck acceleration, bounced around on the balloon tires and headed down the beach. The sudden appearance of the beach buggy sent the sea gulls, feasting on dead fish and plankton, scattering in angry protest.

"How do you like it?"

"Is it far to where we are going?" Rock managed.

"Naw, just ten miles down the peninsula! Best sunset viewing in the area."

"Where is the drawing of the weapon?"

"Dig under the seat for my sketch pad. It's probably there somewhere," the beachboy shouted as he accelerated madly.

Rock did feel something like a pad, and he pulled it out and opened it. He could hardly turn the pages in the wildly bouncing buggy. He didn't want to lose the pad—if it did contain something important—to the gusting wind. He just held it until buggy slid to a halt.

"We're *here*—come on," Murf said, clambering down onto the sand. Rock snapped out of his harness and was glad to set foot on terra firma. Murf started walking toward some blankets and other objects on a small rise of sand near the water. They were, Rockson observed, on a very narrow peninsula surrounded by surf. "Have a seat; I'll find you a beer."

Rockson sat down heavily and opened the sketch pad. There were sketches of fifty-foot waves and whales throwing themselves out of the stormy waters. Murf glanced over his shoulder, and said, "I drew that one in the Mid-Pacific, after a storm. A *mother* of a storm! I was exploring farther out than any of us ever went. Thousands of miles from the coast. I used old maps I found at the marina in Los Diengo — that's a village all collapsed and rotted down the coast, toward L.A. crater. The weather on my trip was great for days then suddenly changed. The winds were typhoon strength for eight days!"

Rock, turning through page after page of sketches of fantastic waves and weird sea creatures, said, "You're quite brave to undertake such a trip."

"What should a man do?" Murf asked. "Watch TV?"

Rock didn't reply, for he had finally come to the sketch he had longed to see. It was labelled "THE CRYSTAL GNAA, AS DESCRIBED BY NATIVES." The sketch was of a spherical, amber crystal with a million facets. Judging by the Polynesian maiden standing next to it for reference, it was twelve feet high.

Rock was surprised. Was this the weapon? The crystal, or whatever it was, stood on a hillock and appeared to be hooked up to a set of heavy electrical cables at its concrete base. There were several drawings of the thing, showing it from different sides. In one picture, you could see it was near a concrete bunker ruin. Then there was a picture Murf had drawn of the empty concrete base and several cables.

"That one," said Murf, glancing over, "is the way it looks on the hill now, with the crystal gone. See the gouges in the dirt where they dragged it away?"

"*Who* dragged it away?"

"Turn the page."

Rock did and gasped. There was a sketch of the face of a gaunt, almost green-skinned man with deep-set dark eyes and dead-rat-colored tufts of short hair. The man had on a high-collar black uniform with death's-head insignias on both collars.

"*Killov!*" Rock gasped.

"The natives say that this man led the Soviet soldiers that dragged the crystal — which the natives worshipped as a god — to a large boat. They said his name was Killalowee."

Killov seemed to exude evil, even in the sketch.

How could it be? It was *impossible,* and yet here was the face. Yes, it had to be Killov — the arch enemy of all mankind: the Skull, the Devastator, the evil renegade, Colonel Killov! So he hadn't been blown to bits in Washington after all.

"I know this man," Rock said. "It is a good likeness."

Rock's eyes narrowed in hate and awe. Couldn't anything kill The Skull? Was he doomed to forever seek to destroy this evil that haunted the world? Was Rockson doomed to confront Killov *again and again?*

He was now *sure* the crystal was indeed a weapon. A most deadly weapon. "Where did Killalowee take the crystal?"

"No one knows," Murf said. "He headed south on the big ship it was loaded onto — after his men shot many islanders. Killalowee had something like an armed whaling boat, near as I could gather from the native's descriptions. The soldiers hauled the crystal overland on cables and slid it onto the ship's ramp, the natives said."

"Just like Killov," muttered Rockson, remembering the oil tanker Killov had once converted to a death ship filled with weaponry to attack Washington. "His name is Killov, not Killalowee. They also call him the Antichrist, and Death Incarnate. He is the man who destroyed the best chance for a peace between East and West. We thought he was dead so many times. He must be stopped!"

"All men are conquerable," said Murf, flexing his muscles. By now, the sun was low and red. "Isn't it awesome? Come on, *lighten up* man — this is California. Let's open a few beers and get comfortable — that's my religion. I worship fun and comfort."

"Very traditional American," said Rockson, only half in jest. "We're a bit stoic and spartan ourselves back in Century City."

"Tell me about Century City."

Rockson carefully closed the sketch pad and placed it on the beach blanket. He started to explain the beauties and wonders of his home base, but hadn't gotten far when there was a roar. Rock turned and saw several dune buggies coming down the sandy peninsula. The first one was wiggling wildly, bouncing almost out of control. The bearded driver stood up and waved.

It was Archer!

"Archer, slow down," Rock yelled. "You'll run us down!"

The big mountain man managed a sand-throwing

wheel-about just a dozen feet away as Rock prepared to sprint toward the water.

Archer clambered out, "Wheeerree steamers?" he demanded. "Big hungry!"

The rest of the gang arrived shortly with the Surfcombers. Murf dug up the clams and steamers that had been heating in the sand-covered charcoal fire near the blanket. He had set them baking earlier that day. He passed them around on red plastic plates, with some beers.

"Mmmm," said their trail cook McCaughlin appreciatively. "Great! But could use a bit of my patented creeper-vine juice!"

McCaughlin fished in his worn backpack and extracted a labelless green bottle. "Right from the steaming jungle craters of radioactive Utah," he said, "and packs a wallop."

He spritzed a few drops on his open steamer and swallowed it. "Deee-LISH," he exclaimed. McCaughlin suggested they all try his seasoning, but there were no takers.

After the meal, they sat back full and fat and satisfied.

"Sunset!" Knudson exclaimed.

Rock watched as the Surfcombers bowed to the pale ochre disk hitting the water. Then, as the sky darkened, Rockson told the gathered Freefighters what Murf had said to him about Rarapani and Killov. "We have to go to the island," he said, with grim determination. "Somehow we have to find out where Killov went and stop him."

"Tall order," muttered Detroit. "But I have a gre-

33

nade with Killov's name engraved on it in my bandolier."

"AND I HAVE ARROW WITH NAME!" interjected Archer, not to be outdone.

Rock turned to the chief. "Do you have any large boats, something bigger than the skiff Murf explored with?"

"Do we *ever* man!" the chief exclaimed proudly. "You come with me—you must see our great ships."

Chief Knudson led Rockson at a fast pace back up the spit of sand and then down over several dunes, explaining as they walked. "There is a neat little bay over here, where we anchor our twin ships."

They climbed a steep dune. The Surfcombers' yellow eyes, Rockson realized, were obviously a night adaptation. If it was not for the white shirt the Surfcomber chief had slipped on, Rock would have been unable to follow him in the pale crescent moon's light. As they crested the big dune, in the phosphorescence of the sea ahead, the Doomsday Warrior made out the twin sails of two bizarre outrigger canoes. Each canoe was the size of a small cruiser, easily ninety feet long. Their shiny metal hulls glinted like sea diamonds. He whistled.

"Yeah, they're beauties, ain't they? And the sails are not just for wind, they're solar powered, too! There are wind lulls for days in the South Pacific, you know." He led Rock down to the surf, and they waded out and boarded one of the ships via a rope ladder.

Rock was amazed at the sleekness and clean lines

of the ship's design. He walked slowly down the polished deck, taking in every exquisite detail.

"Best of ship crafting," Knudson said proudly. "Combines ancient and modern. Computers, all that stuff aboard for navigation. This ship is called the *Muscle Beach*. The other one is the *Surf City*. We named them after our ancestors' hangouts. We can leave for Rarapani tomorrow, if you want. I assume," he said, "that you want our help?" There was excitement in those big yellow orbs.

"That would be fine," Rock said, sliding his hands over the polished mahogany of the helm wheel. "Tomorrow . . ."

He stared out at the waves and the stars appearing above them. Again, Rockson thought, the bony hand of Killov beckoned him into a new adventure.

CHAPTER 3

After a good night's sleep back in the beach shack, Rockson and his men went down to the twin, sail ships where the Surfcombers had been loading supplies since dawn. They had donned white uniforms, and natty white sailors' caps adorned their blond heads. They looked competent.

Rock pushed a reluctant Archer up the *Muscle Beach*'s gangplank, which had been lowered to the beach. Rock had asked that Knudson load aboard as many of the packets of high explosives used on the power-tridents as they could spare. He saw the chief of the Surfcombers approaching from the ship's bridge to greet him. "One hundred and eighty pounds of the explosives aboard, plus the weapons and supplies you requested."

Rock realized that the Surfcombers weren't nearly as laid back as they pretended. They must have been up at the crack of dawn to get so far in loading the two ships.

Murf handed a ship's manifest to him listing the

correct assortment of supplies for the trip, neatly checked off.

"The *Surf City* has a 12 man crew," said Murf. "We will have the Freefighters, plus 6 experienced crew members: Knudson, myself, Salty, George, Alf and Sammy. Knudson's our captain, Manny captains the *Surf City*. We old salts will be needed to train you and your men as sailors. Plus we'll teach you trident throwing; you teach us use of your weapons."

"Good. I'm very pleased," Rock replied.

"We get underway in twenty minutes—with the flood tide. Sudden waves will flood the bay. Best have all your men hold on tight to something."

Sudden?"

"Don't worry. The ships are pointed to sea. We'll raise the sails and start tacking out the minute the waves hit the bows."

While Archer and the other Freefighters were drafted for various labors on and below deck, the chief showed Rockson the gyro-compass in the Masters cabin below the foredeck. "Ever handle a sailboat or a Sunrigger canoe?" he asked.

Rockson had to admit he hadn't. He had never been to sea, as a matter of fact. "I'll catch on. . . ."

"Sure. You don't look like a landlubber. It isn't hard, if you have sailor legs on you. We'll train you as first mate while we sail. If you don't catch on right away, don't worry."

Knudson went over the ship, explaining the sails and their functions most completely. "Know the sails and you know the ship, my friend. There's a foresail and a mainsail—plus we also have a big spinnaker we unfurl in good weather. Now, sails operate in a different way than most people think. You can actually sail directly into the wind, if your design is right."

Rock heard a warning siren go off on the main-mast.

"That's one minute to wave," Knudson said. "Here, grab one of the brass grips. They're all over the ship!"

Rockson, as they were near the high bowsprit of the sleek white-painted *Muscle Beach,* could see the green line on the horizon.

"Oh — my God, that wave," Rockson started, "is — "

"Coming straight at us," the chief said. The siren was now warbling on and off. "Ten second warning!"

The waves was obviously many times the height of the ship, and still gathering. The noise it made was more like a thousand freight trains than a wave. It just *kept growing!*

"Oh . . . *shit!*" Rock said.

The tidal wave hit the bowsprit with an impact that nearly knocked Rockson off his feet. But he felt an odd, rapidly rising feeling in his gut, like he was going up suddenly in a high-speed elevator. There was a torrent of spray, and when he wiped his eyes, he saw they were moving forward at a fast clip. The sister ship of the *Muscle Beach* was alongside them, riding majestically, its bow pointed high like a speed-boat in the blue-green water.

Rock turned aft and saw that the beach they had

39

just left was under water. Even the dunes beyond it barely showed.

"Some tide," he said, prying his left hand off the brass rail. "How'd we manage to crest that wave?"

Knudson laughed. "It's all in the design—and timing. Our pontoon—you'll see it riding low in the water fifty feet to port—is the secret. It helps lift our keel right up out of the water when the big wave hits.

"The outrigger design was invented by Polynesians, who made long ocean voyages before western man built his first rowboat. The advantage over standard design is obvious—balance and flotation in big waves. We have made some refinements to the ancient design, of course."

"My skiff was an outrigger, too," said Murf, coming up alongside them. "It weathered every storm, like this ship will."

"We have a good wind," Knudson said, "so my crew will let up the spinnaker." Knudson started shouting orders.

Rock watched as waterproof bags were snapped open and a giant billowing sail was lifted on high by a crew of six handling the ropes—aided by Archer. The blue sail billowed out full, and the ship gathered speed. In the distance, the *Surf City* also unfurled an orange-and-red spinnaker.

Rockson was amazed at how the big ship skimmed along the water, like some jet-propelled craft or a hydrofoil.

Murf stood proud and tall at the helm, steering her through what he said were dangerous reefs and sandbars. For the next ten minutes Rockson watched him work. Rock saw no reef in the murky green water save once, and then he was thankful for the narrow gauge of the ship — and Murf's skill — as they rocketed past it.

Once in the open sea, in bright sunshine and modest waves, they settled down to a routine. Flying fish and dolphins trailed them; it was all sunny and beautiful. As the first day went on, there were lessons for all the Freefighters on various aspects of ship life. Archer was set to learning knots from Salty, the rather acerbic older Surfcomber with the peg leg. Rock studied navigation with Murf; Detroit was put to study the riggings and sails; Scheransky was shown the auxilliary engine and the life-support systems. Chen and McCaughlin drew the less glamorous jobs, assisting the crew in cleaning decks. Then there was weapons' practice — for hours.

First supper aboard was a treat. Murf used a careful, long throw of a trident to spear a large flying fish in mid-leap.

"Sushi!" exclaimed Archer when, with pike and net, the Surfcombers pulled the beauteous flying fish on deck.

"You got it, Archer" — Chen laughed — "the ocean is teeming with delicious things." He slapped the gentle giant on his back.

After a flying fish and sea scallops meal, they continued their training. Later on in their journey, they would switch jobs, and by the time they got to Rarapani, hopefully the Rock team would be all-around sailors.

Well, Rock surmised, maybe with *one* exception. Archer, when the waves built up on the second day, appeared a bit *green*. They soared through swell after swell, up and down, up and down. The huge mountain man barfed over the side several times and spent a lot of time in the head. But Archer came around by the time the day was over. He even started to gesture animatedly and show them all the knots he had learned to make from his peg-legged instructor.

Life aboard a sailing vessel was a new and thrilling experience for all the Freefighters.

Archer was displeased when they were unable to spear more fish for several days and soon took the fishing upon himself. Archer sat in the stern's bolted-down chair, strapped in place, his steel cord muscles at the ready, holding rod and reel. "Fish no problem," he bragged, "meee strong!"

"If I'm right," said Murf, "the fish *will* be a problem. But since you're eager for supper, play out some line!"

He gave Archer instructions about not holding on too hard when he had a bite, to instead let the 4000-pound test line play out to tire the fish. But Archer, Rock knew, was too impatient to follow such advice. The mountain man planned to just haul the fish in, no matter how big it was!

At about four that afternoon, the boat suddenly lurched under Rockson's feet, nearly throwing him over the low railing into the water. He recovered and realized what it was—*not* a sandbar in open ocean! The wild and angry cry from the stern *said it all:* the mountain man had caught himself a fish. Rockson saw it fly up into the air as he made his way astern. It was a giant swordfish, bigger than Archer and Rock laid head to head.

Archer was all red faced and gnashing his teeth, refusing to let out any line.

Detroit ran to the embattled giant and insisted, "Let out line or I'll keelhaul you—understand?"

Archer had no idea what keelhauling was, but it sounded ominous. Besides, the giant was wearying of holding tight. Archer let out a few hundred yards, and the reel smoked with the speed of the supranylon cord unwinding. For five hours, he battled the swordfish until finally it was limp and alongside the boat.

They let down the dinghy to help load the swordfish up onto the deck. It was a thousand pounds at least. Enough food for the crew for a week.

"Arch, do you want to scale her and I'll cook her?" McCaughlin said.

"MEEE CATCH—*YOU* SCALE!"

CHAPTER 4

Each evening, when everyone else had retired to his sailors' hammock below, Rockson studied the sea charts by flashlight. He had formulated a theory about Rarapani. He was sure that the atoll was really the legendary Johnston Island, an ancient U.S. military installation. That explained the bunker fortification and maybe a lot more — like the crystal weapon. What better place to deploy a strange new weapon than a remote military island? But the description of the island baffled him. *Two* volcanoes — a large *verdant* island. That wasn't Johnston Island, unless a lot had changed. The nuke war had spawned great earth changes. Perhaps, he reasoned, the volcanos were new. Murf had said that they both belched smoke and fire, so they were probably recent additions.

Rockson, on his lonely watch, had little to do but theorize. The helm was lashed on course, and the computer made the small adjustments to their path that were necessary from time to time. He was alone on deck, in utter darkness under a star-filled firmament. Alone, it seemed, in the whole, flat, water world. Horizon to horizon, nothing but ocean — and it would be this way for one more week. At least.

Man is so alone, he thought, as he listened to the creaking of the ship's rigging. Then he saw the twin sails of the *Surf City* some miles distant, heading on the same course, and felt a bit less lonely.

Rock went to the panel beyond the helm and took compass readings from the illuminated globe of the computerized gyro-compass. He had to hand it to the Surfcombers for their space-age equipment.

He sat at the desk by the compass, laid out the sea charts and, taking the readings, used the ruler to draw their path. Four days out now, and less than one-third of the way. The world was big, and yet he knew it was just one of seventy million earth-type planets in a galaxy wheel of ten billion suns. He turned off the small plotting light and laid back on the cool deck staring up at the sky.

What were they *doing* up there? What were all those people on all those worlds doing? Were they voyaging across their own oceans, or making love to their three-eyed women?

Rock tried to be still and fill with the essence of the universe as the Glowers — the isolated race of glowing super-beings — had taught him. He fell asleep after a while and did not wake until the white pearl sun was coming out of the turquoise-blue waters.

The crew sang that day and every day thereafter. They sang ancient sea chants, accompanied by the concertina wielded by Knudson. Perhaps it sounded so wonderful because of the vast loneliness. On some night watches, Rock could hear similar songs wafting on the wind from their distant companion ship.

The idea of having two vessels so far apart was that if one fell into some danger, perhaps the other would be far enough away to avoid it, and yet come to the rescue.

"Columbus used three vessels to get to America and made it back to Spain with just one," Murf explained.

"I trust the method," Rock said. "We call it backup."

At 12:15 P.M. on the eighth day out, they heard the radar's urgent warning buzzer.

"What is it?" asked Detroit. Murf went to the instrument panel and studied the readings. "Bad news, crew. It's a big storm. We must head into it and ride it out—can't outrun it." The bronze sailor looked grim. "This will be a mega-storm, Rockson," he said, drawing the Doomsday Warrior aside. "I don't know if . . ."

Rockson, understanding his meaning, said, "Then let's get to work to improve what chance we have. How long do we have before it hits?"

"About fifteen minutes."

"Drop the spinnaker; get with it!" Knudson was yelling. As the crew did this, and a multitude of other emergency tasks, the sky became ominously grey. The dolphins that had been their ever-present escort dropped beneath the turgid sea.

Everyone quickly donned yellow rain slickers and hats.

The sky was broiling now with black sodden clouds; a burst of lightning rent the heavens. The storm began pouring a torrent of water down upon the craft and its awed human cargo. By the time the last hatch was battened down and secured by heavy ropes, the crew members had trouble seeing in the darkness and heavy rain.

Rockson had been through mega-storms on land before, but this one was the first he had ever encountered at sea, where there was no shelter! Soon the waves were building to fifty-, sixty-, and seventy-foot heights, and the *Muscle Beach* was tossing and rolling like a cork in a mad child's bathwater.

No one could doubt that the very survival of the ship was doubtful. Life or watery death was now up to fate. Murf grabbed Rockson and screamed in his ear over the howling wind. "Someone has to watch the helm—the computer is set to always head directly at the winds. It's sealed from the weather; but *if* it gets wet, it will short out, and the ship could turn sidewise to the waves. Then we'd capsize."

"I'm your man," Rock volunteered. Together, they locked arms, took some heavy rope and attached themselves to the mainmast. If the men were pulled from the depressed cockpit that held the helm, they could work themselves back to their place. This was a precaution that paid off three times in the ensuing hours.

The computer *did* short out when a titanic wave

washed across the deck, submerging the entire vessel for some thirty seconds.

Murf was slammed so hard against the mast—though he wasn't lost overboard thanks to the rope—that he was unable to manage the wheel. Rockson had been aiding Murf in his turning the helm, and now he had to direct the ship all by himself. The effort was too much for any one man—*except* the Doomsday Warrior. For hours he struggled until the barometer began rising and the sky was grey, not black, once more. Then Rockson, pummeled by wind and rain, utterly exhausted from twisting the wheel against its doom-desire, passed out.

Rock's eyes opened slowly. He saw nothing but deep blue. Was he dead? If so, what was this rocking? He realized the blue was sky—clear sky—and that he was flat on his back. He tried to sit up, but his numb arms were lashed to a fallen mast. Next to him Detroit lay, facedown. The black Freefighter was also obviously alive. Rock could hear his intermittent coughing. *What happened?*

Rock remembered now. He had collapsed at the helm as the storm was abating. Then why was he tied?

A shadow blotted out the blue sky while a smell of damp bearskin and muscled sweat filled the air. A big candy-eating grin surrounded by a tangle of red-and-black-streaked beard stood over Rock. "Archer!" Rockson exclaimed. "Did you—"

"MEE MAKE KNOTS GOOOOD!" the gentle giant boasted. He untied the Doomsday Warrior, then helped Detroit up.

Over cups of hot coffee, Chen related how, one by one, the crew, realizing Rockson was unconscious at the helm, had gone topside and attempted to reach the helm to assist. Archer had been the only one to reach Rockson against the wind. He had lashed him down and also tied all the fallen men he could to whatever was handy, so they couldn't wash overboard. "I'm sorry to report that three men — George, Sammy and Alf — died. Washed overboard."

Rock nodded, then looked around. The boat was listing; its masts had been snapped — but she *was* afloat.

"No sign of the *Surf City*," Detroit said glumly, surveying the horizon in a 360-degree search.

Rockson continued to check the damage: no drinking water, and old Salty had a broken arm, which Chen had set already in a splint. The explosives, plus the ammo the Surfcombers had supplied, were lost.

Murf, once recovered, had gone below. Now he came upstairs. "We've stopped taking on water. We'll stay afloat. The gyro-compass still works, Rock, and the helm responds, if a bit sluggishly. If we can rig one mast, we can use wind power."

"Where are we?" Rock asked.

"Miles off course," probably," Murf said. "We should find out."

Soon Rock was taking a compass reading and checking the charts. He was not pleased with his results.

"We're five hundred miles off course—and the nearest island with fresh water is a hundred more miles off course, due east."

"But we've got line and tackle," Murf said. "We'll get fish oil to drink, and we'll eat."

They held a small service for their three lost seamen. Then they silently prayed for the crew of the *Surf City*. Rock wanted to believe they, too, were alive.

"We won't find out until we reach—*if* we reach our destination," Knudson said.

Rock nodded. The odds were against the *Surf City*. The *Muscle Beach* had barely made it through the storm.

"Archer, remind me to sponsor you for Century City's first maritime heroism medal," Rock said, after the service.

Archer's chest swelled.

"*Nothing,*" he said, clearly and softly, "Me *friend.*"

CHAPTER 5

Using only the patched sail of the restored fore-mast, they made slow but steady time, heading for an island marked on the old chart only as "F-2: *uninhabited, contains fresh water.*"

They had rationed their supplies carefully in case they were becalmed, but the westerly winds held, and they were closing on F-2 by the afternoon of the second day post-mega-storm.

The lookout, Scheranksy, called out from the bowsprit. "Ship ahoy, Captain."

"*What?*" Knudson was incredulous. "Is it the *Surf City?*"

"*Nyet*. It's—well, *come look!*"

The captain and the Doomsday Warrior walked up the leaning deck. Rock took the telescope from the Russian's outstretched hand. Once he had the object in question in the lens, he whistled. The unexpected ship was a three-master. "An ancient sailing vessel," Rockson exclaimed, "in very bad repair. The sails are torn; it's listing badly to port and covered with some sort of green vines."

"I didn't believe my own eyes," Scheranksy said. McCaughlin cursed loudly. He had been taking depth readings, dropping the plumb line and calling out the fathoms. Now, suddenly, he had trouble pulling up the sinker. Rockson turned and saw the man yanking with all his might and pulling up to deck a swarm of tangled seaweed. It was like coil springs, thick and pungent. Flopping out of the tangle were small fish and crabs.

"FOOOODDDDD," Archer said proudly, picking up a crab by a claw and dangling it in Rockson's face.

"Never mind that, we'll get trapped in this seaweed like that old ship!" He turned and yelled to Murf, "Astern at full speed."

The *Muscle Beach* slowed to a standstill, then started veering about; yet perhaps it was too late. "If the rudder gets caught in that stuff," Rock uttered, "we're finished."

Murf tied the helm, then came over, leaning over the side alongside Rock. They beheld a green carpet, undulating like a living thing. The *Muscle Beach* suddenly jerked to a halt. A buzzer sounded, and the Surfcomber said grimly, "That means the propellor is fouled. Looks like we're in it pretty bad."

Rock agreed, "This stuff is like a floating flytrap for ships." They both stared at the tangle of vinelike seaweed.

Scheranksy had been sweeping his telescope around from the bowsprit and shouted, "Rock, there are *other* ships out there, too. An old aluminum-hulled cabin cruiser, a battered steamship — and they're all slowly rotating clockwise in this tangle."

"It's like the *Sargasso sea,*" Murf gasped. "If we don't get out now, the ship will be drawn into the vortex!

"Sargasso sea?" Rock asked. "What's that?"

"A cemetery, a trap for ships. I though it was just a tall tale, a legend."

The crew worked like mad to free the *Muscle Beach* for the next forty minutes, but to no avail. Helplessly they drifted into the spiralling seaweed trap.

"The ships don't seem to be moving anymore," Scheranksy stated after climbing down from his perch.

"Don't feel too cheery about that," Murf said, "because it means we're rotating in the vortex *with them*. It will take a lot more than sail power to pull out of it now! Even if we *can* cut free of the weeds."

Detroit said glumly, "Don't count on that. The seaweed stuff is coming up like vines toward the deck—like Rocky Mountain creepers! We're being sealed in."

"What's that over there?" McCaughlin was pointing to the south. "Looks like an island."

Rock took the scope from Scheranksy and focused in. "No, it's another ship. But it has a flat top—and some rusty stuff on deck. . . . *Good God,* there are planes on the deck! It's an old aircraft carrier."

"A carrier?" Scheranksy blurted. "Is it—Soviet?"

"No, relax, it's a derelict. Vintage Third World War, I suspect. I can't quite make out the name on the stern. U.S.S. *Nim*—something . . ."

"Are you thinking what I'm thinking, Rock?" Chen asked.

"If you mean there might be supplies — some more explosives, even canned food and water on the carrier — the answer is *yes*."

"Fine idea," Detroit chided, "but how do we get there?"

The Russian provided the answer. While the others were talking, he had climbed down the side and had gingerly taken a first step onto the hard-packed bed of floating seaweed. "Rock," he shouted now, "the seaweed's so thick, you can walk on it!"

"*Careful,* Scheranksy," Detroit cautioned, "we'd never find your Russian ass if you fell through that stuff."

"Get back up here, on the double!" Rock commanded.

The Russian clambered back aboard, sheepishly saying, "Sorry Rock, I just thought . . ."

"Well, I guess you proved we could actually *walk* to the carrier — if we're careful. And we can explore the other craft, too," Rockson added hopefully. "We might find a more seaworthy vessel than the *Muscle Beach* out there."

Detroit objected. "You really think we can follow Scheranksy's dumb example and simply walk across the seaweed?"

"Yes — with some sort of safety platform along, just in case the slimy mass gives way. We'll fashion some sort of raft, carry it with us. If we start to sink in, we'll get on it, quick."

"That is a good idea," said Scheranksy. "I'm glad I

56

think of it. We did that on the Moscow River one fall, when the ice was not yet firm! I remember—"

"*Later* with the reminisces, Ivan," said Murf, "let's figure out how to build that raft."

In an hour, four of the intrepid American explorers—Rockson, Archer, Murf and Detroit—had walked on the carpet of seaweed far from the *Muscle Beach*, five hundred yards at least. They carried a lightly constructed, six-by-six plank raft between them, one American at each corner. It had been built from the loose deck boards of the *Muscle Beach*. Rock didn't like damaging her further, but it was necessary.

Rock turned to look back. Their pathetic, little ship's stubby mast could hardly be seen above the green rolling seaweed carpet they were traversing. They moved onward across the surreal seascape. Though there were few holes in the sea carpet, once they were in the thick of it, Rock cautioned, "Don't walk in step. We can start a wave motion, and the ground—if I can call it that—will start undulating."

Their first target was not the carrier, but the closest wreck—the *Sally Ann* according to the weathered name on its stern. It was a twentieth century luxury yacht.

When the men set their safety platform down on the weed bed and started climbing her, a flock of sea birds nesting in the rotting superstructure took flight.

On the deck, they beheld crumbling skeletons.

One had a captain's hat on its skull—the hat's cloth nearly gone, but its plastic brim intact as new. Some of the other skeletons had small seabirds' nests in their round, chalk-white, eye sockets.

"There's lots of good aluminum plating here to repair the *Muscle Beach*," Murf exclaimed, pleased at this early result of the journey.

"Funny," Detroit noted, "I don't see why the hell the skeletons didn't rot away. This vessel is about a hundred years old, judging by the design."

"Maybe the air here is full of minerals," Rock offered. "The bones are calcified."

They pushed aside a crumbling door and lit a flash to check the engine room. The engine was a pile of rust—once a gleaming diesel engine, but now of no use. In a few minutes Detroit had noted all that was useful on the craft, and they were on to the next destination—the three-masted sailing ship.

As they approached the brooding hulk, Murf said, "It—seems evil. I don't know why." He was not the only uneasy one. Rock had an eerie forboding but kept it to himself.

An old hemp-rope ladder was dangling invitingly from her aft, and testing it and finding it sound, first Rockson and then the others went up to the ghostly ship's deck.

"It's in remarkably good shape—too good," Murf commented as they headed for the bridge, across creaking deckslats.

Rockson halted as they approached a pair of picniclike crew tables on the aft deck.

"My God," Rock exclaimed, "there's porridge still

smoking hot on the board tables! And hot steaming coffee in the mugs!"

"Ghosts?" asked Archer, dry-mouthed. Rock didn't answer.

"Rock," Murf said, wiping off a brass plate on a door, "this ship is called the *Flying Dutchman!* It's the cursed ghost ship. Let's leave — now!"

"Not so fast," said Rock. "Someone lives here on this seaweed ship. They aren't ghosts, either. Probably want us to think so. It's got stores aplenty-I'll bet. The name on that plate is probably just to scare boarders away."

"And doing a *good* job of it," Murf said, nervously looking around. "If it's not a ghost ship, how come it's almost like new after three or four hundred years?"

"This ship's wood," Rock said, bending down, thumping on a plank, "is hardwood and has simply calcified, hard as metal, like the stuff on the *Sally Ann.*"

"Great," the beachboy said, "but nevertheless, let's get the hell out of here before the ghosts or *people* that made the coffee come back!"

"Okay, okay! First we see if this ship has anything we need," Rock whispered.

"You bet," Detroit said, lifting up his twin .44s. "Ghosts or men, I'll blast away anyone that tries to stop us!"

To Rock's disappointment, an hour's search of the craft revealed no supplies of worth — and no phantom crew, either.

An hour's farther walk and they were at the

59

aircraft carrier. It was surrounded by a thinner carpet of seaweed that smelled real bad, and was colored brown, not green.

"Why are the weeds dead?" Detroit asked.

"I can guess," said the Doomsday Warrior, "it was exposed to radiation. This carrier probably is a nuclear job. The engine might be leaking radiation. Let's get aboard—but via the foredeck. The brown area is mostly at the stern."

They had to have Archer fire a grapple arrow up, as there was no ladder. They climbed the sturdy line, one by one. The deck was a rustling mass with many holes. Rusted planes sat like mummified ducks farther down its flat surface.

"I bet," said Detroit eagerly, "that we'll find some ammo here to replace the stuff lost in the storm."

Rock had the men split up, cautioning, "Report back here in an hour."

"If I see ghost—I *yell,*" said the mountain man.

Rockson was the first back. He had some good finds: a sextant and charts. One by one, each member of the exploring team returned with his own pile of goodies. Detroit had found some pistols—well oiled. "They were sunk in grease, we can just shine 'em up. They'll be good as new."

"I find ammo," Archer said proudly as he came out of the gloom.

Archer set down two heavy, black metal satchels. Rockson pried one open and exclaimed, *"Plastique!*—Good man, Archer. We'll blow the *Muscle*

Beach free of the weeds."

Murf returned looking shaken to his bones. "I found wet footprints! A dozen—or more. Bare feet! It must be the pirate ghosts from the *Flying Dutchman!*"

"No," the Doomsday Warrior said. "Whoever the hell they are, they are flesh and blood humans and—" Rockson froze in mid-sentence, for out of the corner of his eye he had seen one of the sacks of pistols that Detroit had gathered slither away, pulled by an unseen hand. The sack rounded a corner and disappeared.

"There *is* somebody here," Rock whispered. He rushed to the corner and caught a fleeting glimpse of something fast moving and grey darting down the deck toward the rusting planes.

"What did you see?" Murf asked, coming alongside Rock.

"Looked like a dwarf!" Rock took out his balisong knife and pursued, the others following. When they reached the rusting jets, they saw lots of small skeletons scattered about.

"Kids?" asked Detroit.

"Maybe . . ." Then Rockson saw *them:* stunted, twisted little men in tattered sailor's outfits. One was limping away with the bags of pistols he had reclaimed, whimpering in fear.

A dozen other miniature beings skittered out from holes in the planes, snarling like trapped rats. One of the super-fast creatures caught its foot in a collapsed piece of rusting airplane and jerked to a halt. Now they got a chance to see what one looked like.

It was a pathetic creature, human but full of sores and spotted with tufts of grey hair. Its nose was big and sniffing, the nostrils flaring; its eyes were tiny cataract-filled things.

"It's nearly blind," Detroit said.

His voice caused a panic in the creature, which jerked on its leg and, snarling and yipping in fear and anger, tore free and ran for it.

"My God—mutant humans!" Murf said.

Detroit raised his guns to bring him down.

"No," said Rock, "don't shoot. I think these sad creatures are fellow Americans!"

"What?" Detroit gasped. "Those little ratlike things?"

"I found out the name of this carrier," Rock said. "It is an American ship. This is the U.S.S. *Nimitz;* these sailors are *Americans*—forth or fifth generation living in this Sargasso-like sea—they just probably want to be left alone. They could have shot at us, you know. And they didn't."

Detroit put his weapons down, stunned." The radiation did it, I suppose."

Rockson wanted to get back to the *Muscle Beach* by dark. They had materials to patch her hull, and charts, explosives and other items they needed. Time to *move on*.

CHAPTER 6

At dawn, they made good use of the explosives Archer had found. Rock had them set the plastique at intervals all around the ship. When they were detonated and broke up the tangle of seaweed, the repaired sail was raised, and they tacked slowly out of the seaweed sea. It took several sets of explosions to completely free the ship.

In sunny weather, they headed on — not toward the fresh water island — for they had found that the tubular seaweed they exploded contained ample fresh water, which they drained into barrels. Instead, they limped toward Rarapani once more. As they sailed away from the seaweed, Rockson resumed his solitary night watch on deck. He thought a lot about the poor blind scurrying wretches aboard the *Nimitz* — one of the saddest post-nuke races he'd ever encountered! There must have been women sailors on the Nimitz to procreate. Then the odd seafood, isolation, radiation — all had combined to leave their great grandchildren the warped, frightened creatures that they were. The journey weighed heavily on him.

The Rock team had gone through a lot already: one ship and all hands probably lost, three of their own crew dead, and they hadn't even reached their first stop. Maybe this time the cards were stacked in Killov's favor.

By the seventh day after leaving the "Sargasso," they had less than a hundred knots to go if Rockson's calculation were correct. He was using the sextant to take bearings on the sun and stars, while Murf was plotting their course on the old carrier's charts. Plus he verified the readings with the battered gyro-compass.

There was a squall on the eighth day, but the restored and fortified *Muscle Beach* made it through handily. They even rigged a small second sail, thus taking advantage of the gusty winds to get ahead. When the clouds broke before dawn on the ninth day, Rock was gratified that they had kept on course. They passed a little island called Atu-mara according to the ancient maps, confirming their good course.

The tenth day was utterly still, and they were becalmed. They used the partially functioning solar-power converter to make a few knots an hour. At dusk they saw two odd, brown cumulus clouds on the starboard horizon.

"What do you make of that?" asked Rockson, handing the scope to Murf.

Murf replied, "Well, it *could* be the smoke of Rarapani's twin volcanos. Or that could be a bad storm brewing dead ahead."

"Yeah," said Rock, cynically. "In which case we'd better tack away."

"Your decision, Rockson," Murf said.

After a few minutes of trying to get a feeling — danger or not — from his mutant senses, Rock announced, "Let's take a heading toward the clouds."

In an hour they were rewarded with the shout of "Land-ho!"

"You sure, Archer?"

In his best tremulous bass voice, Archer said, "MMMEEE SUURRE!"

"Yes, it's definitely the twin volcanos," said Murf, climbing up onto the rigging next to Archer. "Congratulations, Rockson, you're right on course!"

"The congrats are for me and you Murf. The way you and I work, we should open a navigation school!"

They tacked their boat in toward the palm-covered shore. Soon they spotted a dozen war canoes with huge dragon-carved bowsprits heading their way. The telescope revealed the canoes' crews: comely maidens, bare chested and vigorously rowing.

"We're here — Rarapani," Murf exclaimed happily.

"Better than that," said Rockson. He had swept the telescope along the palmy atoll. "There's the *Surf City* — safe and sound in the harbor! Both her masts are intact . . . and look — she's firing up a welcome flare!"

"Ahoy!" came a muffled shout from the lead canoe. "Request permission to board."

Murf took the scope. "My God, it's Manny! He's

with the natives!"

The bulky Manny, now quite a bit trimmed down by the ardure of the voyage, was the first to board the *Muscle Beach*. He excitedly greeted one and all. Manny had thought all hands on the *Muscle Beach* were lost!

Murf explained about the three crew members lost, and then about the seaweed sea. They broke open some beers Manny had brought along and drank toasts for each of the departed.

"How long have you been here, Manny?" Rock asked.

"Three days. The natives are, well, spectacularly friendly. Especially the women, as Murf said."

The war canoes were all pulled alongside now, and up the ropes came Murf's special girl, Mirani, who threw herself at him passionately. They excused themselves for a bit in the below-deck privacy.

Rockson, Knudson and the other men got into the canoes with the giggling island girls and headed for the beach, their necks strewn with leis. On shore, Rockson saw that there were men on this island, too, but many less than women. The men wore short-cropped hair, had wavy dot-pattern tattoos and were muscular and deeply tanned. They each carried something that looked like a combination small boat paddle and bludgeon of heavy carved wood. A formidable weapon, but not against Soviet bullets.

Murf explained, "The Reds wiped out more than half of their menfolk. There's a shortage of men on the island — all the more reason we're welcome."

Suddenly all the islanders parted way. A tall figure approached, masked in multicolor feathers. Her long jet-black hair was arranged in a halo of a hundred pigtails, tied with tiny shells and feathers. She wore a jacket of blue cowries and beads. Only by her shapely legs and her gait did Rock know for sure she was a woman.

The masked woman came over to Rock and tentatively touched the white streak in his hair. He felt a sudden electricity as he let the strange creature do so.

"Pretty, pretty. I like," she said.

Rockson had been told that the natives spoke pidgin English and was please to have it verified.

"I like you eyes," she said. She lifted one of her several shell necklaces over her head and placed it on the Doomsday Warrior. Then she left them, disappearing in the foliage.

"Ho, Rockson!" Murf laughed, "I think you're being pursued already." Rockson and the other men each had several girls clustered around them as they crossed the beach toward several large thatched huts arranged among the palms. In front of the huts, elderly people in blue flower-pattern sarongs were beating drums of welcome.

"WHOOOOO IS THHHATT?" Archer pointed with much excitement. His enthusiasm was usually reserved for food, but Rockson, following his gaze, saw an immense rolly-polly native woman crashing through the grass.

"That's Hohanna," said Murf. "Just your size,

isn't she?"

"MEEE LIKE!"

Rock winked when he caught Murf's eyes. Archer stepped forward from the group of men and stared at Hohanna, who froze in her tracks and smiled shyly at him in return.

"My God," said Murf, "they're both petrified pink at the sight of one another. They're—stupefied."

"Mesmerized maybe is a better word," Rock added. "I think it's love at first sight."

Later, as twilight set in, a large, succulent island boar was turned over a roaring campfire. A feast had been laid out in the village of thatch huts and longhouses for the adventurers. Archer and many of the other men had paired off with native girls. The mountain man had the seat of honor next to Chief Umauu because the chief's oldest daughter, Hohanna, was sweet on him.

"See," Murf said, slavering down a dollop of poi, "Hohanna feeds Arch from her own bowl!"

Rockson worried. "He won't run into any sex taboo or something, will he Detroit?"

"Hell no," said the team anthropologist, who sat next to Rock on his other side opposite Murf, "the native women are free and easy about such things. They've thrown off more than the bras that the missionaries foisted on them! They've restored their nature gods and destroyed the churches and the sex taboos of western man. I've been asking questions," Detroit continued, between bites of hot pork ribs, "and discovered a lot. For instance, they call the nuclear war '*when-the-western-god-turned-on-the-white-man.*' The natives, being so isolated, were not killed, though they heard much of the world was gone. They concluded their saviors were their gods-of-old. So we're back to the way things used to be on this island and all over the Pacific — pure Polynesian!"

Rockson, when Murf pointed, turned to see Archer being trained to eat lobster correctly by Hohanna. "He usually eats the shells. It makes a *horrible* noise." Rock laughed. "Maybe she'll tame him."

The food was delicious and plentiful, but Rockson soon put it down. A beautiful creature — the epitome of female Polynesian beauty — came ambling toward them. *"Who* is that?" Rock exclaimed.

"That's Leilani again, Rock," Murf said. "You know, the feathery one that likes your hair?"

The saronged beauty squatted down in front of Rockson on the colorful blankets, amidst the fruit and meat plates. She smiled and started feeding him pieces of sweet-baked breadfruit.

"Leilani," encouraged Murf, "is just your type, don't you think, Rock?"

Rock's heart pounded as he stared. The legs were the same. She had brushed back that tangle of black hair into a silky bun, tied with sea fronds, and removed the feather coat. He beheld true beauty, beauty which didn't stop at the figure, like most of the island girls. Leilani had a beautiful *face*, too!

He took a morsel of meat from her tan outstretched fingers, and she smiled a perfect white-toothed grin.

"Gonna be fun for you tonight," Chen said, mockingly.

Rock nodded, mesmerized by the dark doe-eyes of the island woman.

CHAPTER 7

Murf told him he could expect the beautiful Leilani's visit, but Rock, to his great surprise, had a night of uninterrupted sleep in his small hut. Over a breakfast of ship's-store coffee and fried breadfruit, the other men boasted of various nocturnal pleasure visits by the island girls. Rock was silent.

Detroit called him aside, explaining, "Rock, your girl Leilani—she's—well, I found out she's a high-priestess . . ."

"So?"

"So she's—a *virgin,* Rock. And has to *remain* so. Don't mess with the local customs, that's Century City's prime order you know."

Rock frowned but nodded. So that was it!

Detroit said, "Murf tells me the chief wants us to wait for the propitious day tomorrow before talking business. Today we're supposed to enjoy."

Leilani showed up to "help Rock eat" lunch, and then they went down to a lonely part of the beach to

71

swim. They stripped off their clothing and stood looking out at the waves. Leilani had on a bikini-type bottom of some sort, made with beads and shells, and nothing else. Rock was very turned on. She said, "Surf not high on this side of island—and water no shark."

He wanted to hold her to him but would not try. There was a very gentle childlike feeling coming from Leilani—not a sexual feeling. She was so damned innocent, he wouldn't push it—yet. He brushed her hair back and said, "You shouldn't hide your beauty." He stared at her dark eyes and high-cheekboned Polynesian features. She pulled away, laughing, running into the crystal-clear water. "Want to get pretty shells," she implored, "then you follow me! We make necklace at my hut."

"Sounds good," Rockson said, imagining seclusion with Leilani. Eagerly he dove into the lapping surf beside her.

They pushed down below the surface into a silent beautiful world of shimmering colored, mirror fish and corals. The bottom looked like a fantasy realm, too: beautiful mother-of-pearl, lustrous shells, castlelike coral. An undersea paradise.

She touched his arm and directed Rock's attention to a particular bed of seashells. Oysters—large, colored-shelled oysters. They gathered some and broke for air, then gathered again, each time depositing their booty in a net bag that she tied to a driftwood log on the beach.

Once they had gathered enough, they went ashore. Rock broke open several oysters and slavered them down.

"Hey," he exclaimed, biting into something hard. He pulled a black pearl — worth maybe ten thousand dollars — from his mouth.

"Throw away," she said, "it *bad*. Most these oysters good taste but have bad things in them! Only thing black things good for is girl use for necklace." She spat one out, making a face.

"Leilani," Rock asked, "are there little black things like this in *all* these oysters?"

"So? Who need them, 'cept for necklaces. Coral make more pretty color necklace and bracelets — not so common!"

"These are rare and expensive in the outside world," Rockson said. But after a while he too spat them out like Leilani did, leaving them on the pristine sands of the paradise beach.

Rockson was hot for Leilani, and he saw the same look in her eyes; but he was worried about the consequences for the mission if he let his control go.

Later, Rockson tracked down Murf at the chief's house. "Take a walk with me," he urged. As they walked on a jungle path Rock asked, "What else do you know about Leilani?"

Murf said, "Leilani is the priestess of the Cult of the Gnaa — a virgin chosen from one 'pure' family line. By pure I think they mean psychic. Leilani *has to* remain pure. Don't push her, Rockson. She is one of the keys to getting help from the native chief. These natives are friendly, *if* you don't abuse their beliefs and gods."

"What's this Gnaa?"

"That's actually their name for the crystal weapon, Rockson. The natives worshipped it. Leilani was the priestess that performed rites at its site."

"I see," Rock said, thinking that Leilani could be a source of information about the crystal that he had to plumb.

Rock spent the evening with Leilani—hands off—attempting to draw her out about the Gnaa crystal. They spoke little, creating a silent empathy. They had an uncanny ability to sense one another's thoughts. Rock had some ESP ability and was sure hers was far stronger. He could feel her *desire,* too, her warm femininity. He wished to hell she wasn't a virgin priestess!

Rockson and Leilani walked the beautiful orchid-laden paths of the island, communing while the others repaired the *Muscle Beach* with the aid of the natives. He asked many questions.

Leilani explained her ESP. "I have what the island people call 'knowing-of-what-is.' My duties to the Gnaa were the pouring of ablutions on the set of shrines on Mother and Father Fire mountains."

"Mother and Father Fire—oh, the volcanos."

"Yes, the volcanos."

"I want to see where the crystal—the Gnaa god—was located," Rockson asked her. Her wide pupils shrank in fear.

"No, that place is taboo. Only I go to the sacred temple area. No man, no girl, can go there—taboo. Only Leilani go there—at round moon—and I then think on crystal, sit still, smell flowers. Then after hour, the power comes, the 'knowing-of-what-is' in my head—no explain possible. My mind of pure crystal glow like blue moonstone. The island rejoice, for I have power. I high priestess, I *power-woman!*"

Stopping, he held her arm. "Leilani, we can get the Gnaa god back—if you help. But I *must* go to where it was located before Killalowee came."

After a long time, she sighed. "Killalowee already break taboo. Okay, you will see—but after purity water. You bathe in sacred fountain first, and I give you cowrie shells to adorn your head like Leilani has."

Rock found himself being led to and immersed in a bubbling, warm blue lagoon under the full moon. She placed the cowrie crown on his black locks, and she smiled. "Now you sacred, too. Come to temple with me, Priest of Gnaa."

He couldn't help it. He moved to kiss her, and she obliged. "I like this thing you call *kiss* men do with other girls! I wish to lay down with you, too, but I am the Gnaa priestess. Pure . . ." She looked sad. *"Come. Come."*

They set out for Mother Mountain in the moonlight, having dressed in white robes. Rockson, as they climbed, felt the gentle touch of Leilani's mind on his. She climbed rapidly ahead, then waited for him, silhouetted in the windswept gossamer gown against the yellow moon—a vision glowing with untouched sensuality.

They were soon lost in the white mists of the barren pumice slope.

They reached a ledge about fifty feet wide. "The volcano is quiet now," she said. "She likes you—accepts you." She laughed as the Father Mountain belched a plume of smoke. "The Father-of-mine is less sure of you. Look—" She pointed to the lava flowing red on the far mountain. "He will see you good," Leilani encouraged and pulled him onward, even higher. Rock hoped she knew the path very well, for he could hardly see to walk.

They then came to an area with huge totemlike poles; the mossy terrain here was scarred with huge truck-tire gouges.

"This was sacred, beautiful," she said, "but now much destruction."

They moved on to a flagstoned area, and Rock stumbled on a copper cable. He found that it issued from the ground itself and ran to a circular, raised area of concrete. There he found more torn cables. It was just like in Murf's sketch. Something big had been in the center of those clipped cables!

"This is where Gnaa—you call crystal—stood," she lamented.

Rockson examined the cables. Where had the power come from? The ground—Of course! Geothermal source.

"Where's the blockhouse, Leilani?"

"Over there." She pointed higher. He saw a square shape silhouetted against the stars. "I'll look at it next."

"Wait, Rockson," she pleaded. "Show me the kiss again, and I tell you something important."

"I'm willing to be bribed," he said, "for information." He kissed her long and hard.

"Well?"

She smiled. "I can tell you where the Gnaa went!"

"Where?"

"Far—over there." She pointed at the sea. "I have a feeling for crystal." She stood, her hair streaming in the wind, her bare feet secure on the pumice. "It calls to me from that direction."

Rockson carefully noted where she pointed. To the west, down the atoll's reef. "Another island?"

"I feel yes," she said, hesitantly. "It—the Gnaa—misses me."

"This blockhouse—" Rock said again, "I must go in it and see what I can learn from any writings from the past inside. It could help me understand the Gnaa and its power."

She nodded. "That is place of your race—not mine," she said. "You go alone. *That* place taboo even for me. I wait."

CHAPTER 8

Rockson climbed toward the rectangular block-house. At first it was easy, as there was a gouged path made by many booted feet. He soon came to many rows of warrior graves marked with long staffs of hardwood carved into elongated likenesses of nature gods. These noble natives had fallen fighting the well-armed KGB soldiers. Then he came upon a rusting military half-track. Rock brushed the volcanic ash off its door and found what he expected, the red skull and crossed swords emblem of Killov! The vehicle was standing half on its side, its track twisted off. He pulled the door open. There was a skeleton inside, wearing rotting military garb. The uniform was black, high collar — definitely KGB.

Where does Killov get his volunteers, Rock wondered. Why do they follow a man such as he? Perhaps the promise of glory. . . . No: *power* . . . that's his recruitment bait.

A worm inched out of a round eye socket and fell onto the boney fingers, found a bit of flesh and began to eat it.

With disgust, Rockson slammed the door on the

dead man and made the last part of the climb.

The blockhouse was windowless, its walls pitted and eroded by over a century's weathering. It was covered with vines. He had to grope around two sides until he found an *open* door.

Killov's men had been in there! The door had been blown off by a grenade or shell. Rock feared that they had taken what he so needed to find—a record of what the crystal weapon was and how it worked.

He entered, found a Soviet chem-flash on the floor and tried the switch. It worked. Rock shined the beam around, over rusting file cabinets, old smashed desks, collapsed shelving and smashed, ancient, radio equipment.

He pulled a few file drawers open—nothing but rotted fragments of paper, disintegrating at his touch. His heart sank until he spotted the video screen in the corner. At first he thought it was a TV. Then he realized it was an old-style monitor. For a computer! And computer meant disk memory. Frantically he searched for a disk.

On a nearby desk, Rockson found a broken-open strong box marked SECRET.

The disks were in Killov's possession.

He despaired, again, until he saw a rusting metal door—leading to a cellar? He broke it open and, flashlight in hand, went down several twisting steps. Rats hastened away; a snake slithered into a recess. Rock was undeterred. His boots were tough and his mutant skin more impervious to such things as rat and snake bites.

He entered a low-ceilinged dank cellar. Gingerly, he opened the dank, crumbling file cabinets, looking for a duplicate hard copy of the missing disks.

He found a plastic-sheathed copy of a report labelled "President's Eye's Only," and snatched it up. He broke an ancient seal and saw the heading ULTRA TOP SECRET. PROJECT ZILCH. Was that the name of the installation—or the weapon?

As he sat on a rock outside the building, reading each plastic-sealed page, Rockson felt like he was prying into a forbidden part of history. He'd often had that queasy feeling when some new and precious document relating to the final war was in his hands. More than a superb fighter for America, he had become an avid historian—especially since his trip back along an alternate time path.

The crystal, he learned, was part of a larger plan called S.D.I.

S.D.I. involved, it seemed from his reading, ground and sky-based weapons for focusing the gathered energy of geothermal power and then using it on an enemy. The ZILCH crystal was such a gatherer and focuser of power. It was to beam its power to a space-deployed mirror called SATMOS-5. The space mirror hovered over the Pacific at 23,500 miles high. The weapon could zap anyplace on earth with the power of a hundred nuke bombs!

He put down the document halfway through. Would the mirror satellite still work? Yes. There is no decay in space!

Rockson read on.

There were codes in the book for moving the mirror satellite into position, but that page was partly eaten away by the years. Damn! If only Killov's stolen computer disk had such a flaw in it!

But it didn't. Killov wouldn't have bothered to load the giant crystal weapon on a ship and lug it away if he didn't have the activation codes. The crystal had to be found and destroyed, or awesome destruction would be unleashed—destruction that would make Killov the dictator of the world!

Rockson read on with morbid fascination. The engineering and in-orbit deployment of the folded metal mirror was accomplished by secret flights of the space shuttles *Discover* and *Reliant* in the 1980s—under cover that the satellite deployed was a spy camera satellite.

The difficult work of creating the crystal—the most powerful neuro computer diode ever brought into existence, a trillion trillion memory bits—was detailed. He learned that the crystal weapon carried, stored and amplifed energy through each of its complex molecules. This cybernetic-energy breakthrough was accomplished by a team of ten thousand U.S. scientists isolated here on Rarapani for five years, under tighter secrecy than that of the Manhattan Project.

Rock was aware that most of the world was starving back in 1989, and yet the immense technical feat was undertaken. Imagine, he thought, if all that ingenuity had been spent on solving the world's political, economic and social problems back then.

A nuclear war could have been avoided.

Mankind could have reached for the stars — instead of Star Wars.

He quickly flipped through the rest of the 230 pages, found there was a personal letter dated July 8, 1989, marked ULTRA SECRET EYES ONLY, Senator Harkings, from Captain R.C. Tempos, Commander, Project 43.

Rockson read:

The ZILCH crystal is an utterly new weapons technology: the U.S. is way ahead of the Soviets on this one! They haven't even, as far as we know, *conceived* of such a device.

HOW IT WORKS: To put it in layman's terms, the ZILCH builds up a charge from its geothermal power source. It holds the power in the same way electricity builds up on a ballon when rubbed. Then the immense power is concentrated and beamed up to our space-deployed SATMOS-5 Strategic Defense Mirror, then directed to whatever we wish to annihilate on the Earth.

TESTING: The ZILCH system was tested on August 8, 1989. Results were not perfect, but it demonstrated that with modifications, the ZILCH can be fully operational and ready by November, 1990.

The test shot was aimed at a fleet of dilapidated warships. They should have melted, but the targets were only heated to tepid temperatures. The mirror and the crystal worked perfectly, only there was a miscalculation as to the interference-constant of the Earth's lower atmosphere. The telemetry and other data showed what the problem was—the near-ground position of the crystal dissipated some of the power. The crystal has to be raised above the present altitude. Construction has begun on a 300 meter high scaffold.

Rockson put the folder down. He had enough. The crystal would need a tower to be fired from. That meant wherever Killov went, he would have to build one.

Scheransky had been monitoring world news broadcasts. There weren't any reports of destruction or any ultimatums from Killov *yet*. Killov was probably right now building a tower. Then the madman had to wire the thing up again. It would take months. Plus Killov needed a huge electrical power source—geothermal or possibly nuclear. Where did Killov take it? Where, within a thousand miles, *could* he take the crystal where he would have all that power handy? It was a jigsaw puzzle of death that Rockson would have to solve in order to let the world survive for a few more years.

Rock shoved the red plastic-covered file in a bag he had found in the blockhouse and headed back down the slope to Leilani.

CHAPTER 9

That night, after Murf had made some laid-back requests to Chief Umauu, the chief consented to discuss the Killalowee problem at last.

The chief would walk with Rockson on the Chief's Path through the jungle. "It's a great honor," Detroit said, "to be invited to walk with him. But be careful not to offend."

Rockson saw the chief approach them from his hut. Umauu thumped him on his chest and said, "So we walk as men do on the islands, slowly, head held proudly high, looking straight ahead; not at one another."

They walked. Rockson observed the no-talking-unless-he-asks-a-question taboo, just as Detroit had coached him.

"Because of your man Archer," the chief stated loudly, "you bring much happiness to my daughter Hohannah. I am told by Murf-man that you big enemy of bad fella Killalowee—this so?"

"Yes," said Rockson emphatically. "I'm plenty big enemy of bad fella Killalowee!"

"This big good," the chief said. He pondered, hands behind his back, for a long while as they walked slowly through the lush moonlit surroundings.

"You have more tobacco?" the chief asked. "Murf-man give me small bag, all gone. You have more?"

"Yes, Chief, we brought you best tobacco of Eastern world — because Murf-man said you like." Rock was getting tired of the pidgin English.

"That good. I think you good all-around fella-men."

"Thank you . . ." Rock said.

"Alright," said the chief.

They strolled on. The parrots were singing night songs and the jungle flowers' fragrance drifted over the paradise path. The chief stopped in his tracks, suddenly angry. He twisted the ceremonial flywhisk in his hand like he was wringing a neck. "Me wanna mess up bad Killalowee!"

"Good!" Rockson picked up. "Me help you. I mess up bad fella Killalowee good! But I need some things from you and your people to do that!" At last, Rock thought, I've made my point.

"Hmmmmm. What you want, Chief-Fella-of-Entire-Outer-World?"

Rock winced at his title. He wished that Murf hadn't built him up quite so much! Still, Rock liked the monicker better than Doomsday Warrior. He had to smile, too, at the thought of how President Langford's face would appear if he heard the elaborate expression.

"I need much men and war canoes," Rock stated. "Me special need big dragon boat."

"Okay, you have. What else?"

Rock had the whole shopping list, and he now rattled the list off.

The chief quickly said he would oblige. "You will go far in water to mess up bad fella?"

"Yes."

"You no take big fella Archer from my Hohannah! Archer stay here!"

"Sorry, Chief, I *need* Archer. He—er—big hero. He best of my men."

"No! Archer stay here. Hohannah need big man," the chief fumed.

"I need big man come with me to fight bad Killalowee."

The chief threw down his flyswat and stood arms crossed. "No! Archer stay!"

Rock wondered what to do. Then he had an idea. Rockson smiled and said to the chief, "I Chief-of-Entire-Outer-World make a deal. My big man marry your big girl before leave. Deal?"

The chief grunted and picked up his flyswat. *"Deal!"*

Hohannah was "much sad" when she heard that Archer was to leave. But her father told her Archer would marry her—tomorrow. Then she was happy and jumped up and down clapping her hands, creating a minor earthquake.

Detroit was told the news, and he went to Rockson. "You really did it now, Rock," he complained. "I don't think Archer will go for it, even if it is a big honor to marry the chief's daughter."

Rockson smiled halfheartedly. True, the big guy didn't like strings attached to him. He was the ultimate freebooter, not even associating with the other warriors of Century City—except on missions. Archer preferred his own wanderings, his own company. But it was the only way Rock could get what he needed!

"I suppose I'll have to tell him," Rock said.

"NNNNO!" Archer moaned. "OHH NNOOON-NOONNOOO!"

Rockson blocked the exit to the hut that the session was taking place in. "Sorry Arch," Rockson ordered. "You *have to* do it. We need the dragon boat and the chief's supplies. Saying you would marry Hohannah was the only way I could get them."

"NNNNOT MARRRY!"

"But you'll be *rich,* Archer," Detroit added, as an inducement. "The dowry is pearls, heaps of gold, lots of land . . ."

Archer chewed this over and then said, "NOOOO! I NEEED FREEE!"

"What are we gonna do?" Detroit, who had come along with his team leader as moral support, asked, throwing up his hands. "The chief will withdraw the dragon ship *and* the men, without the wedding."

Rockson said, "Archer—it's an *order*. You've

braved wind and storm, Russian bullets, nuclear bombs. You bailed out of a Soviet jet at Mach 2; you fought a lake-monster. How about it? What's one simple little-old marriage?"

"NOOOO! NEVER!"

For the wedding, Archer and Hohannah wore the customary Polynesian bride and groom outfits— masses of parrot feathers. In addition, Archer had some small orchids sewn in his beard. There were maids of honor: Leilani and two younger sisters of the chief's daughter. Rockson and the other Freefighters added a bit of chivalry by lining up on both sides of the jungle-clearing aisle and raising crossed swords as an archway for the "happy" couple to walk through.

Archer and his giggling, bouncing bride ran underneath the arch and stood before the chief. Umauu wrapped a rope around their joined wrists and knotted it. The knot, it was said, would not come undone until the bride's passion was satisfied.

Rockson saw the wild look of fear in Archer's eyes as the big man's wrist was entwined with the red vine rope. He sensed that Archer might try to bolt and lifted his shotpistol suggestively, pointing it at Archer's gut. The big man caught the motion, and understood there was no backing out.

It was a *nice* shotgun wedding.

Archer glumly accepted the wrist binding and said, *"Ikiwanapaki,* Hohannah," the equivalent of "I do," and went off with his bride to the wedding hut.

The next day the Americans began outfitting the huge dragon boat for the journey. The native ship was a replacement for the *Muscle Beach* which would stay at the island undergoing repairs. The *Dragon* was twice its size, and despite its fierce ornate bowsprit, Murf pronounced it a "marvelous vessel."

Rockson had to admit that Leilani had logic on her side when she insisted that she come along in the search for the crystal. As a result, Leilani was the only woman aboard.

She would use her psychic gift, her link with the crystal she called Gnaa, to help guide the expedition to the right location.

Rockson tried not to appear glum, but inwardly he believed the whole venture was likely to fail. Even if they found Killov, it was twenty-five lightly armed men — and one woman — versus a reported five hundred well-armed KGBers.

The *Dragon* rode next to the heavily-laden *Surf City* in the bay. At noontide the ships put up their sails. Rockson leaned down over the side of the *Dragon* and shook Umauu's hand as the chief stood at the raised bow of his canoe.

"We go mess up Killalowee, you betcha, Chief."

The chief let out a war cry in response. It nearly blew out Rock's eardrum, but he smiled a thanks.

Hohannah had to be forcibly pried from Archer!

The Americans, plus eighteen sturdy native men set sail. Other Islanders, banging on drums and shouting, accompanied them for miles in their out-riggers before turning back.

"How does it feel to be a married man, Archer?" Rock asked as Archer sat on deck looking dazedly at the horizon.

All he got in response was a low growl.

"*Easy* pal, easy!" Rockson tempered Archer. "It ain't so bad. You like Hohannah anyway—right?"

Archer nodded glumly.

"Sorry for the forced marriage, old pal," Rock said, messing the giant's hair, "but you were the key to getting the *Dragon*, supplies and men. Your *bravery* made this voyage possible. If we succeed in stopping Killov, it will be *you* we have to thank."

CHAPTER 10

Rockson laid next to Leilani on deck that night, listening to the rigging creak, watching the stars. God, how he wanted to make love with her—he couldn't sleep. He tried to hold her once, but she pushed him away.

Just before dawn, there was a persistent slapping sound near the boat, like giant oars. Yet Rockson saw nothing in the water when he got up to look over the side. He shook Leilani awake. "Do you hear that?"

"Yes, of course—don't worry," she assured.

"What is it?"

"That's just our friend Mirogoga—the sea turtle god. He will help us find our way."

"Can you—speak to him?"

"In a way—like the Gnaa, he gives off *feelings*. But I don't depend on Mirogoga alone to find way. The crystal calls, sometimes faint, sometimes strong. The course is still correct. The Gnaa tell me it stand still now, but far, far, away. I always show you way."

"I'll keep us on exactly that course with the navigation devices — the sextant and charts and gyrocompass."

She laughed, "No silly. No outer-world ways are necessary. I know traditional ways. I navigate this way." She touched her nose and looked at the sky. "At night I see three stars — Mira, Depa and Taani. They parade like fire-gods across the sky, always splash down in water at right hand of the moon-god. Of course, the always-stay-still star helps."

"The North Star, Polaris," Rock said, "yes, it always stays still."

"But this is not all my people's pointing-way," she said proudly. "You see the waves? They are different colors whenever they change direction. The season is summer, so a blue-green means they come from straight north. A foaming blue on the very top of wave means it is come-from-south wave. I see with the mind's eye, not the head's eyes!"

"Yes," he said, "the Glowers taught me that way."

"Who are they? They are wise men?"

"It's — a long story."

That first day out, the sun was hot like a fire above the blue water. The Polynesian crew members were in great spirits. "It is said that chief-son on voyage is great good luck," one said, pounding the American mountain man on the back vociferously.

Archer smiled and let rip a giant fart — his only comment.

"That good luck, too!" the irrepressible native added.

94

"Archer—stow it!" Rock snapped. "Good luck or not, don't fart—that's an order!"

Leilani pointed out the flying fish off the starboard, their scales of blue and green catching the sun like sequins on an Arab woman's dress. "See, the sky-fish too give us direction. The fish tell me the bad men came this way."

"How do they say?"

"The way they wiggle, plus—I feel with them. Oh, look—see that foaming place near the ship?"

"I *think* so," Rock replied.

"That's the turtle again. Mirogoga is ancient, older than the ocean itself. He learned to swim from the giants that first swam when the rains fell and made the big pools—before the ocean. The god-turtle want my present!" Leilani took off and threw one of her flower leis in the water. "Oh, Mirogoga, don't fear," she said. "We will not harpoon you—if you show us the way to the crystal, to the island of bad men!"

The third day out, Leilani grew somber. "The Gnaa is closer now, much closer," she said emphatically. "It calls to me, says it is afraid, and that we must hurry!"

"The crystal is *afraid?* Does it think? What is it afraid of?" Rock, despite his openness, found a psychic weapon dubious. "Gnaa fears being used for evil. It knows what is in the mind of the evil man that possesses it."

Rockson chewed on that as dolphins came jumping up high near the ship. Was Leilani imagining all these messages?

Rock kept tracing their course on the maps. He was glad to occasionally see their companion's ship, the *Surf City*, on the horizon, keeping the *Dragon* company.

On the fifth day out, Chen came to Rock as he stood at the ship's wheel. "Rock, you gotta see this."

"What is it, Chen?"

"Just come up atop the mast and see."

The Doomsday Warrior climbed behind Chen into the little crowsnest. He saw on the horizon what looked like an amber, glinting eye high on a lattice-work, metal tower! Rockson's worst fears were realized. "That's it," he mumbled.

"Are you sure it's the crystal?" Chen asked.

"What else can it be?"

Rockson met with Knudson, Leilani and Murf at the helm. They decided to drop the sails and signal the *Surf City* to do likewise. They would wait until dark, then approach Killov's island.

When the sun set, lights came on under the "eye," making even clearer the Eiffel-like spire holding the crystal.

"I can't believe," complained Rockson, "that Killov has already built a tower like that. The evil bastard works fast."

"Or maybe," said Chen, "Killov's found some

ready-made tower!"

On that suggestion, Rock carefully checked the maps. "We're looking at the island of Bikini — does that sound familiar to you, Chen?"

"Yes, it's the place the hydrogen bombs were tested in the 1950's and 60's. The island was so radioactive that the natives who evacuated it for the tests never were allowed to return. It was part of the U.S. trust territory."

"Do you suppose," asked Detroit, "that there was an old nuke test tower there, and that Killov's mounted the crystal weapon atop that?"

"I doubt such a tower would have survived until now." Rockson took up the binocs. He trained them on the ten-mile-distant tower. A thousand electric bulbs on its structure showed its entire three hundred plus meters height. There was a building in its core. As Rock studied it, Leilani cried out, "Oh — PAIN! PAIN!"

"What is it?" he responded, putting the night glasses down.

"The crystal calls to me. It — feels — pain. It doesn't want to be used for death. It says it must *kill*. Soon!"

"How soon?" Rock pleaded.

"Just soon, it says." She slumped, exhausted, in his strong arms.

As the ship edged carefully closer in the dark, they found the whole island ablaze with lights.

"It's a goddamned metropolis," Detroit said, handing Rock the binoculars. "We can bet Killov didn't build all that!" There, a reef — and a bay."

Rock ordered, "We lay anchor. Signal the *Surf City* by semaphor lights. We will send a party ashore in a canoe."

A peaked form like a volcano appeared out of some clouds in the distance. And somehow — it looked *familiar.* "I want a look-see at this island. I want to find out," Rock stated grimly, "What gives *before* we go charging in on Killov."

CHAPTER 11

Colonel Killov got into his black Subaru limosine and relaxed his gaunt frame into the cold leather seat. He had decided to leave the tower and get some fresh air, even if it was cool midnight air. He had been reading the engineering reports for hours, and it made him feel ill. Not because the reports were bad, quite the contrary. The crystal was nearly wired, and soon he would be master of the world! But the excitement was too much. He needed to calm his nerves.

He tapped on the glass that divided his domain from the cramped front seat of the limo. The window rolled down. "Nakashima," Killov said, "take me on a tour of Little Toyko. I wish to see if my orders to restore all the buildings that were damaged in the takeover have been carried out."

"Yes, Killov-san," the muscular, slit-eyed driver said. "Where shall I begin?"

"I trust you, Nakashima, to set the itinerary. You know me well; just end up back here at the tower. I want to see the historic sights. They say that this city incorporates the best of old Tokyo—right?"

"Yes, Killov-san," said the chauffeur, pulling out into the clean, well-paved street, "all *exact* copies of old Tokyo sites."

The strange city of New Tokyo spread out before him — a city of 12,000 souls going about their busy ways in the shadow of New Mount Fuji.

The city was actually only twenty square blocks — a 1990's re-creation of the Tokyo that was destroyed in the Nuclear War. It had been painstakingly constructed by survivors of the sinking of Japan in the war-induced great earthquake, who had sought refuge on the island. Homesick for their land, they had sought solace in this rebirth at the foot of a new volcano. They had lived here, preserving their old ways in peace, until Killov's renegade Soviet army arrived.

Killov had picked this island as his base because aerial recon had revealed the tall Tokyo Tower structure, ideal for his crystal *deathbeam* weapon.

The limo pulled up to a low, tile-roofed temple. Killov, who had become fascinated with the strange mid-Pacific Japanese civilization, recognized it as the Sengakuji Temple where the grave markers of the "47 Ronin" were located.

"Good choice," he said. The driver got out and came around to open Killov's door.

Nakashima went up the flagstone walk to the big oak door and rapped heavily upon it. "Open up," he shouted, "open up for Colonel Killov, ruler of this island. His Excellency wishes to see the temple and the graves. Open up, or face a firing squad!"

There were hurried footsteps inside, and then Killov heard a crossbeam being slid laboriously aside. The door creaked open. Inside, a diminutive bald monk in a grey Zen robe bowed and scraped and bade them enter.

Killov strode in, his blackjack boots clicking on the polished wood floor beams, and Nakashima trailed him. "Can we have some damned light!" the gaunt colonel demanded.

The monk scurried off, and a moment later, several electric bulbs scattered about the wood-beam ceiling came on glaringly. The colonel realized they were in a high-vaulted shrine room. He saw a golden statue of the Buddhist god of compassion "Kwannon" sitting in contemplative passivity at its far end. There were several lit joss sticks smoking in a brazier before it. He frowned. Religion and compassion were nonsense.

Killov looked to Nakashima for guidance. "This way, master," Nakashima responded instinctively, leading the colonel down a corridor. "The courtyard contains—what you seek."

They left the temple by an open rear door and came out into a darkened garden. Killov could hear running water. "The Fountain of Death," Nakashima explained. "It runs to honor the Ronin."

The chauffeur shouted out in Japanese, and arc lights lit up the garden. It was only an acre, Killov knew, but the landscaped garden looked larger. It was cleverly designed to give the appearance of a vast outdoor space. There were beds of delicate small flowers amid a trickling streamlet; the gentle breeze waved flower bushes.

They walked together crunching down a gravel path

around a mossy boulder and came to a set of weathered stone pillars about waist height.

"The forty-seven Ronin's ashes are enshrined in these monument stones," Nakashima explained. "The only things remaining of old Japan."

Killov said nothing. He had a sense of something *beyond* here; a feeling of profundity permeated the silent night air. It was—something he seldom experienced. Yes, *it* was here; that *vibration* that Killov so loved: *The triumph of death over life*. Yes, here in this semi-dark garden, before these monuments to the forty-seven fallen samurai!

He paused to reflect on their awesome deeds as Nakashima told the tale:

"The 47 Ronin were warriors for the Lord Asano Naganoni. In A.D. 1703, their Lord broke etiquette and drew his sword on Imperial ground when he was attacked and wounded by a scoundrel named Kina. Only by ritual suicide could Lord Asano atone for his breach of good taste, and so he commited *seppuku*—ritual suicide. His forty-seven Samurai no longer had a master and became "ronin," which meant "purposeless." They plotted and waited to avenge their master, pretending for months to have accepted his fate. One night the Ronin burst in on Kina and beheaded him and placed his head on their master's gravestone. And of course, because such an assassination was a breach of etiquette—despite being of great honor—they all committed suicide like their master, tearing their guts out with the ritual daggers, then being beheaded."

* * *

"Master?" Nakashima asked, touching Killov's cold left hand, "are you all right? You are so still . . . it's been — hours!"

"I am fine. I was just thinking — about death."

"Good, then now I will take you to —"

"No more tour, Nakashima. I feel — I *actually* feel hungry. I *actually* want food, not more arthomethanine pills!"

"That is good master, for you seldom eat, and one *must* eat to live."

"I know, but I subsist on vitamins and drugs because of my many responsibilities. My work taxes me completely, and so I abhor pausing for meals, Nakashima. But these Ronin, their spirit has given me a hunger."

"Then . . . if I may, could I suggest a typical Japanese Inn — a first-class one of course — for an authentic dawn meal?"

"Lead on, Nakashima," Killov said.

They headed across the garden for the limousine.

Killov felt a great energy and talked to Nakashima as they rode. "Nakashima, you know what I build up there in the tower?"

"No, Killov-san. If you do not wish me to know, I understand. It is a secret, is it not?"

"You are my chauffeur; I need your understanding. I *like you,* Nakashima." He paused. "Nakashima — you like me, too, right?" Killov almost swallowed the words. What had come over him?

"I do, Killov-san."

"I believe you're sincere. If you *do* like me, Nakashima, you're the only person in the world except my mother—until I killed her—who *ever* liked me."

When they reached the Tanpopo Inn, the chauffeur pulled in front, sliding the long sedan into a driveway and stopping. "Shall we go in, master?"

"Yes, quickly! I am famished."

A geisha bowed to the floor at the entrance to the ornate thatch-roof building. Killov had to bend under some black curtains emblazoned with calligraphy and found they were in a pleasant, spacious room with perhaps a dozen tables. The windows streamed with the sun rising over New Mt. Fuji.

Killov smelled something fishy and asked, "Is that seafood?"

"Yes, master."

Quickly seated, they were served a wooden board with many different types of raw fish on rice with horseradish. Killov had no trouble—for a change—convincing his palate to accept the succulent tidbits. He felt like a new man when he pushed the plate away, quite empty except for one small leftover.

"Would you like my octopus sushi?" he offered Nakashima.

"Thank you, yes, Killov-san." Nakashima took it, then poured them each a ceramic cup of warm saki. "To *death*," the chauffeur toasted.

"Ah yes. To death." The liquor burned into Killov's drug-sopped esophagus, mixing and melding with many exotic stimulants. The result was a rush of euphoria.

"Ah, a wonderful liquid!" Killov put his cup down.

"And we have common interests. We understand each other. You, too, appreciate death, the poetry of extinction! I have despaired because death was never perfectly expressed. Then, when you came to me, Nakashima, and offered your services, I *saw* it in your eyes. I saw the appreciation for extinction, the ultimate *way*, flickering there!"

"You embarrass me with praise," Nakashima said shyly. "You are my master—the most excellent master of destruction the world has ever seen. The bringer of the extinction that we all secretly yearn for. That is why I sought you out, Killov-san! I am proud to serve you, and learn."

"I see. Then you, Nakashima, are my only pupil, my only *disciple*. I will make you a Death-Master, like myself. Even *I* need a companion. Hades had Charon, *I* shall have *you*—forever!"

And for the first time in a decade, Killov reached out, not to kill, not to depress a button to send up a nuclear missile, not to squeeze a trigger, *but to touch another human*. His cold, bony hand wrapped tightly around Nakashima's. "Friend," Killov said softly.

"Friend," Nakashima stated, his eyes adoring.

Killov, drinking more saki, now poured his heart out. He related how he had been a hunted fugitive, hiding for a whole year in the Moscow Library, living like a troll among the dusty stacks, doing research. "I knew that research would be the answer. Knowledge is power! And I found what I had been looking for—the secret lost KGB file on the American military base at

105

Johnston Island in the Pacific. I found the secret files on Project ZILCH, the weapon that would be my new servant. I gathered loyal men — ambitious men — for my new KGB force, promising them the moon — anything — to join my cause.

"We journeyed to Johnston Island — now called Rarapani — and took the crystal weapon from the savages there. We came here to Bikini by a whaler. My ship's chopper found this island with its tower and its power source. Soon I will use my weapon to bring death worldwide, to make all nations bow to death!"

"Yes, Killov-san."

"One thing puzzles me, Nakashima. . . . Why did the survivors of Japan's destruction build this replica city of New Tokyo?"

"Loneliness, Killov-san. The volcano — it looks like Mount Fuji. They wanted to feel at home."

"Fools! But the duplicate of Tokyo Tower has been useful. . . . Well, that was a hearty meal — my best in years. Let us walk back to the car. I must see how my weapon is progressing!"

CHAPTER 12

As they turned a corner into wide Takanaga Street, New Tokyo Tower's gridwork of red steel came into view. It was 333 meters high, and dwarfed the Tanaka Department Store's twelve stories. In the center of the Eiffel-like tower was a 60 by 60 foot marble shaft with small, green glass windows — the building that held Killov's luxury suite and his control room. Sparks flared at a dozen points at the tower's apex, below where the amber twelve-foot-high crystal weapon caught the morning sun on its million glistening facets.

Good, Killov thought, the sparks meant the workers were welding the power cables into place.

Nakashima drove to the sand-bagged KGB checkpoint at the west leg of the tower. A pair of spit-and-polish KGBers carrying SMGs, recognizing the car, saluted and waved him on. They knew that the ZILCH crystal was the world's most powerful weapon and therefore that Killov was the world's most powerful man.

* * *

High above, soaring on the winds that were rising from the east, a large peregrine falcon looked down at the two men walking toward the tower entrance. It saw their forms appear and disappear in the lattice work below. Its keen eyes sensed that they were like itself. They were not *prey*. They, too, were *hunters*.

Nakashima said, "See that falcon! See how it flies to its nest in the cornice near the very top of the tower."

"You have good eyes, Nakashima. I barely see it. My eyes cannot take such bright sky."

"It is such a big falcon, and it nests on the tower!"

"Then I will have it *shot*. I will not have a bird interfere—" Killov shook his fist.

"No, don't," the chauffeur interjected, "the falcon is a good sign, a symbol of power for you, master. It won't interfere; it is nesting below the crystal."

Killov smiled. "Is that so . . . a good omen? Then I will let it be!"

They went past the rows of saluting KGB guards and into the marble-walled lobby of the tower. Boot heels clicking on the polished floor, they walked to a bank of elevators. The first brass elevator door was marked "staff," the second "engineers," and the third—the silver door—had no words. Just Killov's death's head insignia embossed on the shiny metal.

Killov twisted his gold key in the special elevator's button. A red arrow lit up above the door, pointing down. The elevator was descending from the 71st floor—his suite—where it always automatically returned.

"Do you go to your control room?"

"No, Nakashima. *We* go to check the work on the roof — a surprise inspection."

On the windy narrow roof, technicians worked feverishly to complete their master's design. They were of two races. One race — the stolid pale Russians in black coveralls — handled the bulky electrical cables and welded the structural steel in place, altering the tower's peak to accommodate the crystal. The other race — the Japanese — was smaller, more delicate. They were the highly skilled technicians in orange coveralls, doing the delicate systems work in many fuse- and transducer-boxes that were dotted about the red-leaded steel frame. Slowly, the Japanese grasped what the whole project meant. After the immense crystal was lifted by cables into its "saddle" ten feet over the core building, and the power-grid laid out, they could tell by the megawatts involved that *such power* could destroy a city.

Now, as the two dozen morning shift workers went about their work with welding arc and wrench, or mini-soldering gun and tweezer, the silver elevator door hissed open.

One nervous Russian welder, realizing that the opening door meant that Colonel Killov was arriving, misaligned his welding arc and shorted out a cable. Sparks flew as he dropped his torch and fell backward onto a pile of circuit breakers. In this ungainly position, bent over the pile on his back, the unfortunate Soviet gazed up at the gaunt pale face of the skull.

Killov intoned, "Are you all right?"

"Yes, thank you." The black-coveralled man twisted and scrambled to his feet and saluted. "I — I'm fine!"

"*Too bad,* clumsy fool!" Killov shouted, slapping him hard. "You destroyed some of my valuable equipment!" Killov eyed Nakashima and winked. The muscular Japanese chauffeur knew what his master meant. He stepped forward, delivering a series of arm smashes that sent the careless man reeling back until he teetered on the very edge of the unrailed roof. Then Nakashima delivered an eye jab with two of his leather-gloved left fingers and kicked the man's feet out from under him with a swipe of his left boot. Nakashima listened to his long anguished scream with a smile. Then, when a dull thud ended the scream, Killov turned. "Any more of you wish to make mistakes?"

Everyone got *real* busy.

Killov walked around inspecting their frantic efforts, taking out a note pad and jotting down the numbers on their coveralls. His eyes narrowed if he saw anything that looked behind schedule.

Overall, he was pleased at the progress; but the wind was getting quite heavy and the fast moving dark clouds above looked sodden. Killov wouldn't let weather slow the work!

"Nakashima, let's go downstairs. I'm sure they'll be assiduous now."

Dismissing Nakashima, Killov put on his jet black

kimono and slouched in his leather recliner. He stared out the floor-to-ceiling window at Mount Fuji steaming and sending down a rivulet of fiery lava in the distance.

What *awful* destructive power, he thought. If there was such a thing as reincarnation, he could only wish to come back as a volcano! But he would have volcanic power in this life, too. The geothermal-generated power that would soon be channeled into the ZILCH crystal would make him a *volcano among men!* He would rule the world from this island. His army of 500 elite soldiers could easily handle the timid people — or . . . could they?

Killov worried. Perhaps the troops were his weak link — Were his men being corrupted by this soft life? The only appeal this culture had for him was the ancient and little adhered to veneration of death. The lure of this island for the soldiers was different, namely the vice of the *Ginza's* "floating world": prostitutes of a hundred varieties, gambling, drugs — all hidden in the night. But vice here was all handled so cleanly and tidily! Just like the Japanese to organize and ritualize sex and perversion! Such simple pleasures for his men seemed no threat. Indeed, it kept his troops happy. But . . . when his soldiers roamed the alleys, were they being subtly imbued with philosophy? If so, they might start thinking for themselves. He didn't want his KGB to become a bunch of damned Zen monks or pacifists! They had to be the backbone of the *vast* army that he would recruit worldwide, once he had demonstrated his power!

He smiled. Why worry? The soldiers had no capability whatsoever to grasp thoughts! The could only grasp *women* or *saki bottles*.

But better to be safe. . . .

He snapped his fingers and a guard goose stepped from an alcove and saluted.

"Sir?"

"Yes, Demitrov. I want you to order my KGB to have no more than two hours a day out of barracks compound when not on duty!"

"Sir!" The guard went off again.

Killov was pleased. That will keep them limited to just a quick fuck — no lingering discussions of cherry blossoms or Zen to poison the mind!

Once the guard left, the intercom that connected him to Nakashima's room lit up. When Killov opened the channel, Nakashima's deep voice came on. "Master, could I see you? I have been meditating upon the words of Mushima, and upon the—*ultimate*. I would like to ask you—something."

"Very well, come here," Killov said, flicking the button on his chair's arm to the off position.

Shortly, Nakashima appeared.

"Well, what is it?" The deep-set eyes gazed unblinkingly at the Japanese.

"Master?" He fell at Killov's feet. "Please grant me one request?"

"Perhaps—what is it?" Killov said cautiously.

"You who understands death, you are my teacher—will you *kill* me and cut my head off . . . when it pleases you . . . *whenever* it pleases you to do so."

"I will," Killov agreed. "But not for a while. I need you."

112

"Thank you, master. Please dismember my body and scatter it."

"I will do so for you my—friend." Still, Killov was unaccustomed to speaking the word *friend*. It sounded strange on Killov's lips, but he was deeply moved. No one had *ever* asked him for death—when they weren't being tortured. "I will gladly do so, Nakashima, my—*friend*.

CHAPTER 13

Under cover of darkness the five persons that Rockson had chosen for the recon mission paddled ashore in a canoe. The five were Detroit, Scheransky—some fluent Russian might be called for—Archer, Murf and Rock himself. Rockson was amazed by how efficiently the Polynesian war paddles cut water and propelled them forward, yet made no splashing noise. The outrigger made it through rough surf an ordinary canoe never would have survived. They pulled it ashore and hid the craft under some fallen palm fronds. They had made landfall unobserved—or at least it seemed so.

"Farther down the beach," Rock said, "I spotted a lone house. We make for the house—try to surprise whoever's inside."

Murf nodded, holding his explosive trident up above the splashing surf. "I'm game." The others, too, voiced their eagerness. They slapped the safeties off on their shotpistols, unbuttoned their knife-sheaths and smeared black masker on their cheeks.

Five minutes later they were outside the darkened cabin.

Archer kicked the roughly cut door off its hinges, and the Americans rushed in with raised weapons, surprising a frail Japanese man in his bed.

To the bare-chested man, the hulking figure of Archer and his violent companions must have been a fright. He got out of bed only to frantically crawl under the straw mattress, whimpering.

Rock's keen eyes swept the single room. Moonlight trickled through two uncurtained windows, giving light. No one else was there.

"He's unarmed — and plenty scared!" Rockson shouted. "Put down your weapons."

The Doomsday Warrior went over to a candle, struck a wooden match and lit it. Carefully, as the warm glow lit up the single room, the man crawled, shivering, from under the mattress. He said something like "Ei?"

"Friend," Rock stated, holstering his shotpistol, "you needn't fear us."

"Engrish?" The man's voice quavered, "You no Soviet? You speak Engrish?"

"Yes. We're Americans."

Rockson calmed the Japanese. Over the next twenty minutes the man — he was a fisherman named Nakai — told about how the Russian soldiers had taken over the city at the other side of the island two months ago.

"Even though there was little resistance, the Rus-

116

sians were brutal. Now they exploit the people there and are doing something bad to the great tower. The invaders have no use for us poor scattered fishermen on this side of New Tokyo Island. Still, it is good a dangerous area of hot lava and pits separate me from the killers!"

Rockson got the amazing story of New Tokyo. Then he asked, "Is there anyone in the city we might talk to—someone who will help us defeat the invaders?"

"The man you want to see," said the fisherman firmly, pointing out toward a window that opened onto a slaggy wasteland, "is Chimura-san. He very old and wise, and he is a member of the city's council. He lives at the first house on the other edge of the wasteland. He even has a secret, large cave you can use. But you must be careful crossing the wasteland, especially in the dark. There are geysers of hot steam, and lava pits there."

He then produced a large folded piece of paper, "I can give you map that will take you safely through the lava field. And gifts for the great walking fish that lives there.

"Whenever anyone go into the lava land without gifts for walk-fish, they disappear! Attacked and eaten! When they are searched for, we find their clothes and sometimes huge fish scales around their bones!" The man nearly keeled over in excitement.

"Hey man, *cool out*," Murf said. "Life's a beach!"

"No, it isn't! If you go through the lava lands, take some of my green tikis. Hang them on the scrap heap in lava land. The great fish accepts these trinkets as

117

gifts. It find them pleasing and does not eat the travelers who bring him such gifts!"

The fisherman went over to and opened a small carved chest, extracting several trinket necklaces. He put them over each of their necks. "Remember, leave these out there, for the great fish — or you will all die!"

"Thank you, Nakai," Rockson said, touched at the man's desire to help. Then he asked, "Do the Russians steer clear of the lava zone?"

"Yes, they only go into bad place when they have to repair big white pipes that bring power from the sub-earth flames into the city."

At the first light of dawn they set out into the lava lands. Soon they came upon giant pipes — thermal power conduits — rising out of the slag and basalt rock.

"So that's where all the electricity comes from," Rockson exclaimed. "Killov sure lucked out to find this island!"

Onward they went, single file, following Nakai's map through a hell-like land of bubbling lava pools and twisted sharp tumulus. Then there was a faint noise, like a snarl or labored breathing. "The *fish?*" asked Scheransky, dry mouthed.

"No, just bubbling water," said Rockson. "Come on!"

Ten minutes later they came on piles of scrap: pipes, old cables, the detritus of civilization. Jutting from the waste were rusty iron rods, and tiki necklaces hung on them, swinging in the fetid wind.

"Let's add our gifts to the pile," Rock suggested, "to be on the safe side. Pretty tikis to placate a walking fish."

"Aw," said Detroit, "I like my tiki. It's pretty."

"Just *leave* it," Rockson insisted, hearing *slithering* noises over a smoldering pile of slag. "And then, let's get going!"

Murf also scoffed, but he put his tiki up on a pole, "Bah, a walking giant fish? There aren't such things in the world. I've been all over. I know. You guys have got to get *laid back!*"

One by one the others added their gifts to the iron rods. When they were about a half mile farther along the twisting "safe" route, Rockson climbed a pumice hillock. It was a bright morning, and he didn't like being out in the open.

They were on target. From the top of the hill, he could see green — and a rambling low house surrounded by a bamboo fence. Chimura's house!

CHAPTER 14

Rockson simply went down and knocked on the door. Shortly there was the soft padding of small feet inside, and it swung open. The man who opened the door was bent and wizened—like a 600-year-old dwarf bonsai tree.

"*Irasshai,*" the old man said softly, apparently not the least bit surprised by the unlikely figures outside his simple house. "Please come in. I am Chimura; remove shoes, take slippers," he said in English.

Exchanging their footgear for slippers was easy, except for Archer. The extra-large American had to skip the slippers. The largest pair would not fit his size 18's. They walked inside, Archer in his stocking feet.

"You are just in time for *kabayaki-ya*" said the old man, gesturing for them to enter an exquisite—if low ceilinged—room. There were many decorative vases and subtle flower arrangements.

"NOOOO CHAIIRS," complained Archer, anxious to rest his big buns.

"Please to sit on tatami mats, near lacquer tables,"

121

Chimura said. The old man seated himself. The others, with more or less skill, also got down and sat cross-legged, thighs under the little tables. Archer had to use his table as a lap tray.

Rockson was about to take a seat to the left of Chimura when the old man said, "No, please take place over there."

Detroit whispered, "He is offering you the place of honor—take it. You will have your back to the *tokonomo,* that little alcove in the wall. You see the twig and the little calligraphy scroll?"

Rockson nodded. He remembered reading somewhere about *tokonomo.* It was the place in a Japanese room reserved for the most beautiful thing: a painting or a poem in exquisite calligraphy; or some subtly-formed twig of pine—the sacred tree. The *tokonomo* expressed some subtle and rare beauty. To be given the place before it was indeed an honor.

Rockson bowed and took the seat.

That formality dispensed with, a kimonoed woman, who Chimura introduced as Reiko, his wife, bowed, left, then came back with a tray of some sort of raw fish on rice—*sashimi.* She put six small servings on a little wooden tray and put one on each of their little tables.

Archer looked at the serving disheartendly. "TT-TOOOO SMALL," he muttered sadly.

"Shhh!" Detroit said. "You can have more later!"

Rock said, "Chimura-san, could we speak on urgent business?"

"Oh yes . . . but first"—Chimura smiled—"we will have tea with our snack. You will be tired after your walk."

Rockson nodded. How long could tea take?

After five cups apiece and lots of talk about the weather and flowers, Scheransky blurted, "Lenin! How long can this go on? Time is wasting. . . ."

Their host looked up, somewhat perturbed. *"Shhh!"* Detroit advised. "Better not offend. In Japanese houses you don't raise your voice; it's taken as a challenge. You don't want to fight this nice man, do you, Ivan?"

Chimura sighed, then put down his cup. "We of the New Tokyo council know of your coming. We received signal from the fisherman's flag that you were on your way. I know who you are and why you've come. And I welcome you as friends.

"We of the council fear that the new ruler of the island, Killov-san, will do something very evil soon. The device he puts atop our tower—"

"Means death for millions worldwide," Rockson finished for Chimura. "And it means the subjugation of the entire human race once it's finished. When Killov's gang was first landing, why didn't you fight? You have many men and some weapons, too, I am sure. It might have been possible to stop the KGB forces then. Why didn't anyone fight when they first landed?"

"Rockson-san," said the host, "the hardest, most painful operation of all is the opening of one's eyes to the true nature of things. All life is linked, and violence begets violence. Contemplation reveals that life is all one's own karma. Life is *our own* subtle illusions, so why fight phantasms?

123

"I contemplate this fact often. In the garden. . . . Let me show you my garden."

"Later," Rock said. "The fisherman spoke well of you. He said you have a large cave—that might be used for a base for our forces. But your property is small. Where could such a cave be?"

Chimura got up stiffly, aided by the woman. He said, "It is large, but it is in my small garden! Come!" He led Rock through a sliding paper door into the house's interior courtyard. The old man waddled on his wooden clogs over to a low, mossy boulder and bent down and snagged a twig.

"Cave is *here!*" He pulled the twig. A hidden door opened. They went down steep steps, then into a narrow corridor.

Rock found himself inside a 100-foot-wide, stone-walled chamber, illuminated by a single huge candle. "It burns for days," Chimura said, "so I leave it lit. The Zen monks meditate here at full moon."

"Wow!" Rock exclaimed. "You could hide an army here! The fisherman was right. This would be a good base of operation. But realistically, from what the fisherman told us about the Soviets being well dug in, a handful of us will not do for an attack. Chimura-san, aren't there any people on this island that will fight alongside us?"

"Yes . . . the Bushido will join you. They wanted to fight before, but we of the council dissuaded them, saying rulers come and go, and that we would absorb and change the Russians. I am embarrassed to say that I myself pointed out that we Japanese feared the American occupation after World War II and were wrong. These KGB have proven different: they brutalize; they mock our institutions; they even chop down our blossoming cherry trees for military barriers. Now that these things have occurred, I will call together the ten elders, and we will vote again on whether to unleash the Bushido from their vow of non-resistance."

"Good. How many Bushido are there?"

"Forty-seven — same as the number of Ronin. A good number, yes?"

"It will *help,*" Rock said, "and with the element of surprise, it might be possible to overwhelm Killov. But how can you hold this meeting under the Soviet's noses?"

"Right here — in the cavern — tonight. The council members are all stooped old men with wispy beards, like myself. We are so old and decrepid — " Chimura laughed — "that they let us come and go, shouting our poetry like Basho! The Russians laugh at us and let us pass. We will meet tonight, and I think the council of elders will allow the Bushidos to join your attack on Killov. I shall raise the red dragon flag atop my house — the council will come."

CHAPTER 15

Rockson was very grateful that the Freefighters had managed to keep hold of three of the little sub-microwave belt radios. One radio was aboard each of the ships. He had the third and used his device to call Chen aboard the *Dragon*. Chen was briefed about what had happened so far and what the landing team had accomplished. Rock ordered, "Get everyone except skeleton crews for the ships here at once — Leilani too. The fisherman will set you on the right path."

Rockson gave standing orders for the crews of the two ships to sail at the first sign of the attack beginning. The ships would come around the island and evacuate the team, once they had blown the crystal from the tower. That was the objective.

Just before dawn, the Doomsday Warrior, watching from a rear slit window in Chimura's house, saw Chen and the others coming down the pumice hill toward the compound.

The newly arriving Freefighters and their Polynesian tribesman allies were led through the house and down into the cavern where a general meeting was being held.

Rock presided, saying, "Shortly the eight-man council of this burg will meet. Chimura promises they will allow a group of their samurai called the Bushido to assist us. My plan is to spend a day here once the Bushido arrives to run through attack plans. Whatever mode of attack we devise, it has to result in using our explosives to blow the crystal to pieces. If the explosion doesn't destroy it, the thousand-foot fall will. There's some stored food and a lavatory in the adjoining chamber. Make yourselves at home. There's an extra pair of torches on the wall."

There was obviously a great lack of enthusiasm. McCaughlin went over and picked up one of the unlit torches, ignited it with a match and held it high. "Give me your tired, your poor muddled asses, yearning to breathe free."

It broke the ice. Everybody laughed, and the palpable gloom lifted.

Detroit spoke up, "Even with forty-seven more men, we're outnumbered nearly ten to one. The power for the crystal comes from the conduits in the lava lands. Why can't we simply blow them up and get the hell off this island?"

"There are a *hundred* power pipes, Detroit. If we blow them, more can be constructed in a few days. The source of power is the island's volcanic core. That *can't* be destroyed. Besides, the crystal has been storing power; that's how it works. No, unless the crystal is destroyed, we will fail to stop Killov."

They all were startled when the stone door creaked open and Chimura, holding a yellowish lantern, descended to join them. "The council is in my house," he reported. "We have all agreed. You may have the Bushido. But there is bad news. The Bushido leader Morimoto has been imprisoned. We don't know where he is. The Soviets have several detention buildings throughout the city. The Bushido will be hard to round up without Morimoto's help, but we of the council will try. It could take days."

Rockson was sickened by the news. Without the Bushido's help, there wouldn't be a chance.

Suddenly Leilani cried out and swooned. Detroit caught her and lowered her onto a blanket thrown down on the rock floor.

They revived her with smelling salts. "What is it?" Rock asked, holding her under her head.

"Oh," she said, "much . . . horror. I feel it—they die . . . horribly, degraded!"

"*Who* dies?"

"Girls—Japanese girls. Oh! Great pain and anguish! They call out to me, to anyone. They plead for help."

"Where?"

"North . . . a big building. At least five floors—strange. Through the power of crystal . . . I see . . . many levels, each with—red roof. Stacked roofs—on one another. I sense ancient wood. Oh help. Help . . ."

Chimura said, "Many roofs? A pagoda! The *red* pagoda! The Russian officers use it as a place of pleasure. They take many women there, and none come out!"

Rock checked the map. Chimura, his face illuminated by the lantern so just his eyes and his white beard were seen, pointed out the pagoda. "The old red temple pagoda is not far from the center of the city."

Leilani sat up, her eyes focused now, alert. "Oh, Rockson, these girls are being tortured! You've got to rescue them."

Rockson didn't know what to say. The lives of a few pathetic captives — was it worth jeopardizing the mission? If the Freefighters went into action on their account, it could tip their hand. As far as Rock knew, Killov didn't even *suspect* they were on the island. . . .

And yet — since the Soviet officers used the red pagoda — maybe they could capture a few, interrogate them, find out Killov's weak points. They *were* short of information. Besides, it would be some time, if ever, before the Bushido could be gathered, and he itched for action!

He sighed. They were caught between a rock and a hard place. Chimura sensed his confusion. "Do the *right* thing Rockson," he counseled.

Rockson nodded. Looked around. "Just my team will go. We will attack the red pagoda and free them."

There were smiles on the faces of all the members of the Rock team. *None* of the Freefighters had been looking forward to days of inaction!

Then, Rock said, "Detroit, I'm sorry. You'll have to stay here and run things. If anything happens to us — it won't — but if it does, carry out the attack on Killov's tower. Destroy the crystal."

Detroit looked glum, but agreed.

CHAPTER 16

At 4 A.M., under the light of a gibbous moon, the five-man attack team made its way along the reeds. The plan of attack was to follow the little stream and stay in the tall grass undetected until they were as close to the Red's Pleasure Pagoda as they could get.

It was nearly a mile of slow sloshing through knee-high water. Finally, Rockson saw the many-roofed tower silhouetted by white steam from the volcanic fissures beyond it.

There was a red dot glowing and fading at the doorway. "That's a guard having a smoke," Rock surmised. "Let's get to him while the door is still open."

He and Scheransky walked right up the sloping lawn. Rockson ducked into some bushes and the Russian continued on, making a lot of noise — as planned. Burping and staggering, singing in Russian, Scheransky made himself obvious to the cigarette-smoking soldier. The guard dropped his butt and took his SMG off his shoulder. *"Stoi,"* he yelled.

"Hey pal — let me in," slurred the Russian Freefighter as if he were drunk. "I, Corporal Scheransky, heard there's some real good stuff in here." He continued forward, and the guard muttered, "Who did you say —"

Scheransky, nearly on him, tripped slightly as if to fall down. The guard started to step forward hesitantly. And he raised his SMG, just in case there was any trouble. But the trouble came *far* too fast for him to do a damned thing about it! As the guard concentrated on "drunken" Scheransky, Rock's arm swung up in a blur from the side. His fist slammed into the man's jaw, knocking him cold before he could shout warning. Archer was just behind Rock, and as the Freefighter leader acted, he tore open the door and rushed into the lit interior. The mountain man grabbed a second guard in a headlock with one arm, and he slammed hard twice with his sledgehammer fist into the fellow's nose. *Once* would have been plenty — since the nose crushed on the first blow into a bloody pancake. The second punch cracked the whole top row of the Red's teeth, so they spewed out like dice onto the hard concrete floor.

"Okay," Rock whispered, as out of the night McCaughlin and Chen appeared. "You two — with Scheransky — will prevent any Reds from coming in and spoiling our party. Archer, you and I are about to become Soviets. *Come on,*" Rock said, "you know the routine."

He dragged in the man he'd taken out and pushed him into an alcove. Archer followed suit with his own, much larger, victim. A minute later they emerged, patting down their Russian uniforms so they didn't look twisted. Luckily the guy Archer had squashed was big—but not nearly big enough. The giant's jacket shoulders burst out, the chest seams ripped from neck to bottom. But they weren't entering a fashion show, they just needed enough time to make those who would stop them hesitate.

They bounded up the first flight of stairs. Rockson swung open a steel door and saw an elaborate dimly-lit Japanese style room. A thin young Japanese woman was chained up by her wrists to a pole just inside the doorway. She was naked as a jay, and her feet dangled a few inches off the floor. Apparently, some sort of "welcome" to those who came inside to sample the building's wares. There were whip marks on her body.

Before he could make a move toward her, a Red came walking in from another room. He saw the two Freefighter's Soviet uniforms, but it didn't fool him one bit. He *knew* the two men who should have been guarding the front of the building.

Corporal Nemovski had been on duty with them for over a month, and damned lucky to get the job—since it meant a shitload of free fun. Seeing the imposters, he dropped his horse whip. The Red's mouth fell open, like his chin was filled with lead. Before Nemovski could utter a word, the smaller invader took one quick step forward, and his foot flew up into the air like a snake striking. The toe of the boot slammed into Nemovski's throat, knocking him backward against the far wall some six feet away. Nemovski slid down to the floor gurgling out his death mumbles as his face turned beet red.

133

Rock didn't even waste the time to see how long it would take the bastard to die, but turned back around to the girl whose eyes had opened slightly from the sound. She looked drugged, her lips hanging loosely, her eyelids fluttering like butterfly wings. Rockson had no idea how long she'd been chained up like that. Pain is a drug, too. But she was there too long.

"Come on girl," Rock said as softly and gently as he could. The girl saw only two Russian uniforms and thought that she was in for more . . . more of what she'd gotten for the last two days. She was beyond really caring now, except that it felt good when the smaller of the two cut her wrists free, and she sank to the ground with a little moan. Rock left her and pulled off the pants and jacket of the corporal sprawled at the base of the wall.

"Here, put these on," the Doomsday Warrior ordered firmly, trying to snap her mind out of whatever hellhole it was in. "Get ready to get out of here. We'll be back for you." Slowly, she moved to comply.

With that, he and Archer started up the spiral staircase that went to the second level. They could hear laughter, moans — and screams. The screams got louder as they rounded the curve of the stairway. Rock motioned to Archer to try to take out whoever they encountered fast and silent. The huge near-mute nodded, and they tiptoed up the creaking wooden stairs that groaned out harshly with every step.

They made it to the second floor door and opened it. Rock edged his head around the corner. A single guard sat about halfway down the corridor, reading. Rockson let the man catch sight of his face, half turned, so he could only see the Red officer's cap. Rock motioned with his arm for the man to come to him and then pulled back. With a curious expression, the Russian guard rose and started forward. He was taking out his Turganev Service Revolver. He walked toward the stairwell and peered around, the pistol at hip level. Suddenly a hand snapped out and grabbed hold of his wrist, pulling him hard. As the Russian flew forward, he was met with a steely fist in the center of his face. That knocked him cold as an ice cube in deep freeze. Rock let the limp body sink to the landing. He pushed it against the wall. The Red sat there as if deep in contemplation, his head resting uncomfortably against the cream-colored wood.

"Come on man — fast," Rock whispered to Archer. He turned right, came to the only room door on the floor and threw it open, jumping inside. The scene inside was nothing less than Rock had expected: three young women, all tied up in odd ways on a table, a chair and a bed. Naked and badly whipped. Welt marks were over their entire nude bodies, their sad brown eyes already having cried so many tears that they were dry now, unable to even shed a single drop.

The two Soviet officers who were standing over the trio, themselves naked, each armed with a long leather whip, looked up at Rock and Archer as if into the eyes of a vengeful set of gods. With expressions of infinite fury on their faces, the two Freefighters came forward fast, each heading for his man. The Reds raised their whips in a futile attempt to stop the attackers — but it was a ridiculous effort. A whip scarcely began descending when Rock's knee went into one man's gut. Archer's hammerlike fist pounded down right on the other Russian's head. His favorite punch, and quite effective. Both of them slid to the floor and didn't move.

Rock and his bearded companion turned back toward the captives, and it was all they could do not to let the tears fall from their own eyes. As hard and tough as they were, there was something about seeing women so tortured, so racked with pain and suffering. . . . They went over to them, Rock talking softly, promising them that they would be all right — that it was over. He cut them free quickly and told them to find the deadmen's clothes or make makeshift garments from the fabrics — and then head downstairs. The women looked at them both with bizarre mixtures of thanks and terror, but they seemed to understand the English well enough. They rose to their feet, half collapsing as their first tentative steps again filled their senses with pain. They hadn't walked for days.

Rock rushed from the room as soon as he saw they were moving, albeit slowly, and he and Archer went to the next level. If the Doomsday Warrior had thought the previous sight was terrible, behind the door of the next den of iniquity was something far more hideous. There were two Japanese women here. Both had little red bumps and craters covering their flesh — cigarette burns! The inflictor of the pain was standing right over both of them as they lay tied down spread-eagled on long pieces of plywood. He was in fact at that moment holding a lit cigarette in his hand and was about to descend to flesh with it.

136

"Hold it, pal," Rock said with grim fury in his shaking voice. "I need a light." Before the sergeant from Minsk could move or say a word, the Doomsday Warrior was upon him like a panther. The man was big and strong, a good fighter. He even managed to get in a punch that bounced off Rock's shoulder, but then the Doomsday Warrior was behind him. He reached out and grabbed the man around the throat and then yanked back hard. He drove his knee up into the base of the spine. There was a loud cracking sound, and then Rock just let the dead thing go. It fell like a sack of sand to the Persian carpet.

So it went as the two Freefighters moved from level to filthy level in the Pleasure Pagoda. Every scene revealed was as horrible as the one before it if not more so. Everywhere, not mere rape and bondage, but torture—with knives, ropes, fire, whips . . . you name it—and the perverted KGB sickos who came there had done it. Rock and Archer took care of every one of the bastards before they could cry out to warn anyone above. They would carry out their crimes no more.

They moved up through each floor freeing the captives and sending them down to the ground level where the captive women were spirited into the reeds by the other Freefighters and given instructions to head back toward Chimura's place. Some had even had the wisdom to organize, taking some of the weapons that they found on the dead guards. More weapons for the assault on the tower!

137

At last there was just a final level. Rock threw the stairwell door open. There was a girl like an angel inside, with a face so glowing and brilliant it was almost hard to look at. She was white as the moon — one of the rare albino Japanese — with purple eyes and shining black hair that hung down over her shoulders to her waist. She was untouched, and by her exquisite beauty, Rockson knew she was being saved for some special officer.

From a shadowed corner of the room, a middle-aged Soviet prison matron, huge and buxom with a thickly made-up face, spoke up.

"Get out of here, you fools. Back to your own girls! She is Major Smernsk's pleasure tonight. He'll use his entire army to find you if you —"

"I *doubt* it," Rockson smirked, pulling the fat madam up by her grey lapels. "Anyway, I'm not the one who's going to harm her. Now get in here," Rock said, forcibly pulling her struggling mass to a closet at the side of the room. "If you were a man I'd kill you, bitch," Rock snarled with disgust. "They'll probably do it for me when they find that your charge is missing." He locked the closet door and threw the key away, then found a window and tore it open. Rockson leaned out, waving his SMG right-left, making a triple crow-caw sound.

From below, McCaughlin responded with the "all's well" — an owl's hoot.

"Come on, baby," Rock said, turning to the little angel who came toward him with open arms. "We're getting the hell out of here." He saw Archer seem to sniff and wipe at his eyes for a second at the scene.

138

Rock scowled at the huge bear of a man as he walked by. "Come on you crybaby, we're not halfway home yet." They headed back down quickly, Rock throwing his uniform jacket over the shivering girl, taking the stairs two at a time. He carried her in his arms. Archer came stomping down behind him like a bull elephant, so the stairs creaked as if they might just give way completely. The entire hundred-plus-year-old pagoda seemed to dance around a little.

The albino girl, who spoke English well enough — English always being the second language of the industrious Orientals — asked, "Who — are you?"

Rock explained breathlessly as they descended, "Americans . . . here to . . . destroy the crystal weapon."

"I — know — about!" she said. "I — can help."

Back on the dark lawn, Rockson — still holding the albino girl — and the Freefighters went for the reeds. "We have to cover our attack," Rock said. "There's some major arriving later tonight — to visit this girl. We have to make it look like something other than a commando raid happened here."

"How the hell do we do that?" whispered Scheransky, swatting a mosquito. The bodies — or, if we could dispose of them, their absence and the missing girls are evidence that someone attacked here.

But Rock had the solution — a violent one. "There won't *be* a pagoda!" he exclaimed. We brought explosives. I'll now tell you why: Chimura said that those fissures steaming behind the pagoda erupted with lava

139

flow thirty-one years ago. Well, they will erupt *again,* more violently, destroying the whole area, pagoda and all, tonight."

Rock told McCaughlin and Scheransky to catch up to the freed girls making their way to Chimura's house. But he had each unload his satchel of explosives first. "Chen," he instructed, "we're going to make it look like mother nature went on a rampage here." He took out the detailed map Chimura had given him and shined the penlight on it. "See these fissures behind the pagoda? We'll drop some of the explosives there, blow 'em open—hopefully they'll spout some lava. It'll work, because it has to!"

The Freefighter sapper team—Chen and Rockson—sneaked back around the pagoda and planted all the explosive satchels in carefully spaced rows along the fissure.

Once back in the reeds, Rock turned the radio-control switch. A monumental series of explosions shook the area. As the two Freefighters ran splashing down the streamlet, geysers of hot water, rock, mud and then molten lava spewed on high. The pagoda, its foundation undermined, leaned like the Tower of Pisa, and then fell into the conflagration.

Sirens wailed in the distance. Chen, glancing to the side as they ran, could see a candy-eating grin on his commander's face, illuminated red by the blazing fury they had left behind them.

CHAPTER 17

The albino girl was named Kimiko. After being taken to the cave and given some warm miso soup, she sat wearing one of Chimura's warm, grey cotton kimonos.

The Freefighters and Leilani listened as Kimiko related what she'd overheard the Soviet officers discuss.

"When I was taken from my parent's home Friday night, I was tied, put in a truck and delivered to the pagoda. I was handled carefully. The KGB team that got me said I was for an important officer. I thought they meant Killov—I feared him the most. I had seen him in a victory parade when he took over the island. He's—like a vampire, so thin—and his *eyes!*

"But the KGB men said I was a present for a Major Smernsk. They snickered about his 'propensities.' I do not know what that means, but it sounded bad.

"They tied me in the top room, the special room they called it. And then they had some drinks with the matron. I was very frightened when they cut my clothes off me. But knives were put away. They sat and drank more. Then they talked about a—crystal weapon."

"What did they say?" Rockson asked, leaning forward.

"Something about the raising of the crystal to the top of Tokyo Tower and—I remember! Yes—a timetable was gone over! One man said that there was just three days of work now and the weapon would be done. Killov would activate the crystal from his suite in the tower's building. It's—the *71st* floor!"

"*Good* Kimiko," Rock urged, "that's helpful. Go on!"

The girl went on—she had quite a good memory. The Red officers had bragged a lot to the matron about their work. There were scattered snatches on positioning of KGB troops—a squad of fifty in each leg of the tower. Rockson took out the map and made quick notes, circling the fortifications she mentioned, in the tower and by the docks. When the girl was done, he was encouraged. "This info," Rockson said, "will help us at lot. Now if only the Bushido would come!"

Killov put down the phone and frowned. He spun the swivel chair and stared out at the glittering Tokyo skyline and Mount Fuji beyond it, like some white ghost.

A horrible natural disaster, Major Smernsk had reported, had overtaken the Pleasure Pagoda. That was what it *seemed* to be! A lava eruption from the unstable geyser behind the Pleasure Pagoda . . . not unheard of on this volcanic island. And yet, Killov was suspicious. Why *now?* Why this time? Coincidence?

He decided to be on the safe side. There might be a resistance movement forming after all. A *clever* one that hid its work.

He picked up the phone. "Search every house within a mile of eruption," he ordered.

"For what, sir?" the corporal on the line queried.

"Idiot! For *anything* strange. Especially for strangers, house guests — anything unusual! Report back to me in one hour!"

All was havoc in Chimura's house as the KGB thugs literally tore the place apart, looking for "anything unusual." Just as they had torn apart the six other houses closest to the destroyed pagoda.

"Stop," Chimura pleaded. "These things are precious! There are many ancient relics, sacred art —"

"Bah — get out of my way you old fool," snarled a thick-set soldier. He smashed Chimura across the face. The old Japanese fell so that his hip struck the fifteenth-century vase in the *tokonomo* alcove. The old vase and its careful O-Hira flower arrangement toppled and smashed on the bare floor.

Oblivious to the flaring pain of his shattered hip, Chimura screamed out, "You — bastard!"

The soldier, who had begun cutting a futon open with a bayonet, turned at the epithet and kicked out his right boot, hitting Chimura in the chest. The snap of several frail ribs caused a paroxysm of pain;

Chimura's eyes rolled up, and he slumped onto the fragmented vase.

His wife was then pulled screaming from the room and stripped. The two young KGBers who did this found Reiko "too old", and shoved her aside, piling broken furniture over her and laughing. Huddling in fear she heard them moving into the bath area. They used their pistols, she could hear the bullets smashing crockery. And then the old woman heard them all trundle out, muttering about the fact that there was no gold for them to take with them. The search-and-destroy was over.

Reiko whimpered for a while then stopped. The only thing that made her stop crying was the fact that the enemies of Killov were still undetected — still safe in the cave. They would strike back at these barbarians!

Rockson and the others heard the gunshots.

"I'll go up," he whispered, pulling his pistol and climbing the stairs. He opened the "rock" a crack and saw the coast was clear. Red dawn spread in the east, sending shafts of color through the bamboo fence. He opened the door wide and went to the house to investigate. Finding the havoc and no sign of Chimura or his wife, he ran back and called for the other Freefighters. They began a search through the house for the missing couple.

"Oh, my God, why they do this?" Leilani gasped.

"KGB are like that," Scheransky said, "filthy pigs!" He lifted an overturned cabinet. "Rock — he's here.

Chimura!"

"Chimura!" Rockson exclaimed, "are you all right?" The man moaned as Rock lifted his head slightly and cradled it. Rockson did his best to comfort the old man, but he was too far gone. He spat some blood and said, "KGB — they — came! Where — my — wife!"

His wife, freed of the tumble above her by McCaughlin, came to him in time to see him smile at her. Then he expired.

She stated simply, "He could not live after *this*. I will help you now — to carry on the attack. Killov must die."

CHAPTER 18

Killov's Afghani bootman slipped the colonel's left boot on and then the right. He buffed them both one last time with his mufti sleeves. This accomplished, the colonel dismissed him. He stood up and called out, "Nakashima! Are you ready?"

"Yes, master," the chauffeur replied, coming out of the adjoining room. He was all spit and polish in a red, high-collar, KGB servant uniform, full of braiding and epaulets. His long dark hair was oiled down, sort of like Valentino.

"You look very good, my friend," Killov said. "Let us now ascend to see how the work progresses!"

Together, they left the suite, headed toward the silver doors of his private elevator. After Killov pressed Roof, Nakashima said, "It was very wise to take the precaution of the searches after the Pleasure Pagoda mysteriously burned. Even if they *did* turn up nothing, it certainly looked suspicious."

"And," said Killov, "it was wiser still to speed up the work on the crystal's wiring. Even if there is no enemy lurking on this island, there is no time to waste in activating my weapon. There is a world to win!"

The door opened onto the dizzying panorama of New Mount Fuji, the emerald and ash island, and the blue Pacific beyond it.

Killov smiled as the men they confronted gasped and/or bowed hysterically. Why were they always so surprised at his presence up here? Didn't they expect to see him *personally* inspect the work from time to time?

"Any laziness will be punished," he called out. Immediately, hammers started banging, welders' torches flaming again. He looked around. "Where is foreman Deminski?" he demanded.

Instantly a black-coveralled, grey-haired, wirey type came up, snapped his heels together and saluted. "Sir! Deminsky reporting!"

Killov's eyes narrowed, "Are you meeting my schedule?"

"Sir!" Deminsky snapped. "We are *ahead* of schedule. If the weather holds, we will be done at noon. But the barometer is dropping. The coming storm threatens to be worse than the last—"

"Despite the weather," Killov hissed, "see to it that the wiring is completed at noon!"

"Yessir!" But there was a hint of panic in the man's voice. The last storm had been a *bad* one! He went back to barking orders, demanding a speedup. Killov watched the officer, pleased. "Perhaps not *all* my men are incompetents, Nakashima."

Killov felt a sudden chill as the wind snapped at his back. He thought his eyes were going bad, too, for it suddenly got very dark. He looked up and saw a black sheath of clouds had cut the sun off. A beautiful morning was instantly funereal-grey.

"Mega-storm, master," Nakashima said. "We'd better leave."

"Sir!" Deminsky pleaded, running over to him. "It will be too windy—we have to abandon work and go below, or—"

"No—keep everyone working! Those who are fearful, *kill* them! They all must know the importance of this project!"

"But the workers—all of us—will be blown off the tower!"

"Bah," Killov scoffed, "you have ropes do you not? The work *must* continue. Nakashima, destroy the controls of the work elevator."

Nakashima took his pistol out of his holster and stepped to the scarred work elevator door. He fired a full clip of 9mm bullets at the buttons, sending sparks and fragments of metal into the air.

The workers all stopped their activities, stunned.

"You will all stay up here until I see the fully operational light come on in my control room," the colonel shouted over the wind. *"Then,* and only then, will I send up my *private* elevator to pick you up!—Deminsky! You heard my orders! Get going!"

With that last order, Killov and his chauffeur stepped through their silver doors and descended, leaving the others to their fate.

An hour later, Killov was rocking back and forth

anxiously in his swivel chair, looking out from the safety of his 71st floor aerie as the fantastic storm clouds swirled. He was *stoned out* on drugs, worse than usual. His veins popped out blue on his thin arms from the arthovalium pills effect, and etherorium-V purple capsules sent thrills of artery-contracting ecstasy in waves up his cheeks and into his swollen brain.

Sheets of rain slammed at the window as lightning rent the sky. Still, the little bulb on his chair arm that was to signal that the crystal was operational didn't come lit. It was 12:10 P.M.

"What are they *doing* up there, playing?" he muttered. "Surely they don't like the rain and wind. Why don't they finish?"

Aggravated with the wait, tired of the rainy view, he decided to amuse himself otherwise. Killov pressed the red button on the control arm of his chair. A whirring noise commenced behind him. He swivelled to see his secret trophy room—the Doll Room— slowly revealed as a bookcase slid back.

Everyone needs a little hobby. Killov's doll collection was a bit strange, but it helped him focus his mind on objectives of long-standing. And his longest standing objective was *revenge!*

He left the seat, walked around his boomerang-shaped, black marble desk and walked unsteadily toward the secret room.

Once inside, he pressed the button that closed him off from view—should anyone *dare* enter his office unannounced!

Before Killov was a display of lifelike dolls on a

long table. These perfectly wrought dolls would be the envy of any child—yet they were not for play in the ordinary sense. They were for *burning!*

Each doll was an exact two-foot-high replica of each of his sworn enemies—those that had stood in his way time and time again—those that had thwarted Killov in his quest for absolute control of the Earth.

The colonel examined them. The *first* doll, Ted Rockson, stood upright, tall and proud. He wore an outfit of khaki green, and an accurate scale model of his Liberator rifle was clutched in his tan, steel-muscled right arm. Rockson had a streak of mutant-white in his long black hair. His eyes were mismatched light- and dark-blue.

Perfect in every hateful detail!

Then there was Premier Vassily, the *#2* doll. Vassily was depicted in a wheelchair made of miniature wires—chrome coated just like the real one. The "Grandfather" wore his eternal shawl over his arthritic shrivelled legs. His damned book of Rilke's poetry was on his lap. He was dozing.

"The peacemaker" Vassily called himself, for now he wanted peace with the U.S. The bastard was as old as time itself, face and hands palsied and covered with age spots, but he just wouldn't die and let a better man—Killov—take his place!

Holding onto the rear of the wheelchair was Ruwanda Rahallah, the premier's black servant and aide-de-camp. The tall Rahallah was the man-behind-the-throne, some said. His very dark figure was accented by the blinding white tuxedo he always wore, and his white gloves. Killov hated him as much as he

151

hated Vassily! The two were inseparable.

Doll #3 was a carefully rendered model of the fat, jowly, bushy-eyebrowed, balding man that was Vassily's nephew, Zhabnov. He had been installed by the premier as the president of the U.S.S.A. He was depicted holding a red rose—Zhabnov's mania was roses! Well, he'd have plenty—at his funeral!

Then there was doll #4—President Langford, the *real* U.S. president. He was sixty-ish, wearing a tan business suit, silver-haired and still looking wan and thin from radiation exposure he never truly recovered from—radiation he'd received from an N-bomb dropped by Killov's bomber!

"Which one?" Killov said, hissing the words between his teeth, dizzy with the thrill of it all. "Which one of you do I kill first?"

He looked at the lined-up figures carefully, staring at them one by one, and then decided: "First you Rockson! You are the most obstinate of these enemies. Then I will do Premier Vassily—and your black lackey Rahallah," he snickered. "I talk to you dolls like you are real—but someday, you will all die for real. Now die in symbolic form!"

He put his hands onto the control levers and activated the little laser guns mounted on the ceiling above the figurines. Killov manipulated the levers until the twin mini-guns pointed upon the first statue—Rockson. The targeting laser lit up a red spot on the lifelike doll's khaki-clad chest. "Now, you obstinate bastard—*die, mutant die!*" Killov squeezed both triggers.

The mini-lasers fired, and light streaked down and

152

ignited the Rockson doll. As the doll flared, then melted and burned, Killov turned the lasers toward Vassily in his wheelchair. The trigger squeezed, the premier and Rahallah burst into flames, too, from the heat of the intense light ray. The realistic metal wheelchair melted, the blanket-shawl smoked and ignited, the plastic faces hung and stretched, then their "flesh" fell off their heavier plastic skulls. The smoke and smell in the room was awful — the smell of burning poly-vinyl — but the colonel didn't care. Killov's drug-crazed senses reeled in pleasure. "Now one more," he said, turning the rays on Zhabnov, with like results.

As the dolls puddled and burned, Killov laughed like the madman he was. He *liked* the smell of burning plastic — or skin. He liked destruction, even if it was just symbolic.

The room's phone started beeping. Killov let it beep. He sat and inhaled the plastic smoke until he started choking; only then did he turn on the vent blowers.

The phone was still beeping, and he picked up and spat angrily, "What the hell is it?"

"Sir!" Deminsky's hysterical voice cried out over a whooshing wind, "the weapon is nearly operational. Please, *please* send the elevator. Don't abandon us, sir! We'll go back to work as soon as the storm breaks! We — we've lost seven men — blown off the — "

Killov snapped, "You *finish!* I'll not have Nakashima send the elevator until the work is done. As for the seven men, there are lots of technical people on this island — we can get replacements easily

153

enough. They should have been proud to die for my cause. Keep the rest working!"

CHAPTER 19

The team had been going over the attack plan for hours.

"There has to be a reconnaissance of the tower before we attack," Rockson concluded. His men, who were clustered around him in the cave, all volunteered.

"I'll do it," Detroit said.

"No me," Scheransky said. "I speak perfect Russian and—"

"Nix! I'll go," Chen insisted. "I have the skill. I can get in and out—"

"I'm going," Rock stated, "with some bugs to plant. But I'll have to wait until the storm is over. Leilani—how about our two ships. Can they ride out the storm?"

Leilani said, "Don't worry. The Polynesians on board will take them into the lee of the island. We have weathered such storms as these, even on the open sea."

"I'm glad you think so. I'm very relieved, then, as soon as it lets up a little, I'll get going."

* * *

At dusk, as the rain died to a mere shower and the wind to a normal-scale gale, Rockson walked out of Chimura's house, dressed as an aged intinerant poet. He wore a whispy white beard and carried a gnarled staff. "One of the best makeup jobs I ever had, thanks to you, Reiko."

She walked him to the gate saying, "But must hide size! There are no aged poets so big." Reiko worried. "Please keep *bent*."

Rock stooped over.

"The stoop is convincing." Chimura's wife smiled. "Keep the paper parasol up — and direct it at the KGB sandbag installations."

Rockson hobbled past his first KGB checkpoint ten minutes later. He was unbothered, except with jibes that he didn't have to pretend not to understand.

The Japanese population was re-emerging into the streets. *They* didn't make fun of his passing. The people loved their vagrant poets in New Tokyo. Rock was assisted across the intersections and greeted with bows everywhere. He didn't know much Japanese, but he had memorized several of the great Basho's seventeenth-century *haikus,* which he shouted out, as if half-batty, at odd moments while he hobbled along:

"With each puff of wind
the butterfly is alighting
differently."

He alternated that poem with:

"By the light of new moon,
the land is inundated
with buckwheat!"

Finally, he had managed to get to a spot right across from the tower. He made mental notes of all he saw but wanted more; he wanted *in*. But how could he get past the sandbags and elite guards? If he ever was scared in his life, this should be the time, despite the shotpistol hidden in his robe. The place was crawling with sullen-looking Reds eager to use their weapons.

Almost forgetting to stoop, Rock started across the still-wet pavement, between slow-moving trucks painted with crude KGB symbols. He was stepping onto the curb in front of the first checkpoint when he heard a click. Out of nowhere, a KGBer had appeared, and Rock now felt the cold steel of a Tokarev pistol barrel on his left temple.

"Old man," the soldier said, "recite a poem to amuse me — or die!" He used English — everyone's second language worldwide since the twentieth century.

Rock giggled and nodded. He hoped the few raindrops still dropping weren't smearing his face-job. This time Rock spat out a verse of the poet Shiki:

"Oh red carnations,
whiteness of butterflies,
who gave them souls?"

When the pistol was removed, Rockson, leaning heavily on his gnarled poet's staff, limped on across

157

the plaza of cut slate.

He was under the grid-work of the Tokyo Tower now, just fifty feet from the ornate gold-leafed double doors of the marble-walled core building, and he didn't have a single idea on what to do now. Except wing it. A truck crawled across the plaza, and at the same time Rock saw a pair of dirty-coveralled workers roll a dumpster out of a service door, spill its contents into a wide pit and roll the thing back toward the entrance. He walked toward them, shouting out poetry, jesturing with his staff. They stopped in their tracks. He was counting on the workers being Japanese, not Reds. Trusting his life on that fact. The truck cut him and the workers off from the view of the guards at the tower's west leg for a second.

"Quick," he whispered to the workers, "I am sent by Chimura-san and the council. I must get into the building. Let me get in the dumpster."

They bowed at the mention of the council. Rock slipped in the dumpster. They kept walking the dumpster—with Rockson in it—back to the service door.

Rock peeked through a hole in the filthy metal cannister. The guards, distracted by checking the I.D. of the truck driver, who they had halted, didn't notice Rock had disappeared. Luck!

Once inside the tower building, he climbed from the dumpster and asked, "Which way to the lobby?"

The pair of stoic workers pointed left toward a door and bowed again.

"Thanks and sayonara," Rock muttered, wiping his grimy kimono off. He must look a mess.

* * *

Just as Rock had hoped, once he was in the lobby, people *assumed* it was okay for him to be there.

Maintaining his crazed-poet persona, Rock limped around, slipping the ten listening devices he had in his robe under tables, in the floral displays and inside the sand ashtray next to the elevators.

He heard a snippet of conversation of two strolling majors: "The colonel will be not pleased that the work crew was blown off the tower. Still, the final switches were put in place."

"Are you serious? Killov will live with a few deaths—as long as the weapon is operational. There's more than enough power to operate the crystal laser now. Tomorrow we rule the world." The officers, using a key, got in a silver elevator, and the door closed.

Rock, muttering koans and haikus, headed toward the silver-doored elevator with the death's head and swords symbol. That would be Killov's private elevator—why not go for the kill now? He was on a roll and should capitalize on it.

As uniformed men passed him in both directions, he pressed his lock pick in the keyhole and twisted. The elevator descended, the door opened and he stepped in. That raised a few eyebrows.

"What the hell is an aged, filthy Japanese doing in Killov's lift?" a startled young lieutenant asked his companion.

"Not our business," the other replied. They walked on, eager not to question the holder of one of Killov's elevator keys.

Rockson's heart pounded as the elevator closed and accelerated smoothly upward. His ears popped at 21, and again at 55. The elevator stopped, and the door opened on 71. *Killov's Lair!*

Nakashima was busy dusting off the dials in Killov's personal control room. Killov had gone to personally inspect the pagoda disaster site, still uneasy about the "freak" natural occurence there, leaving Nakashima in charge.

Nakashima lovingly worked. He'd scrape and bow, even caress his death-master's *boots!* He had learned *so much* about negative energy, about death and darkness from Killov already. And there was so much *more* to learn from the skull.

WHAT? The elevator door was opening. Was his great master back already? Nakashima sensed not and dove to hide in the clothes' wardrobe.

Through the half-shut louver doors, the chauffeur saw a tan muscular man standing over six feet tall and dressed incongruously in tatters of a kimono robe. The man was *very* strange. He had a mane of grey hair and heavy white eyebrows. But it was makeup. He wasn't old at all. Nor was he Japanese! The intruder's mismatched light and dark-blue eyes scanned the room. Nakashima watched as he went directly toward the control panel. The intruder looked around and raised the heavy wooden staff he carried. He raised it over his head, intending, Nakashima realized, to smash it down on Killov's precious instruments.

"Banzai!" the chauffeur shouted, snapping his knife from its belt scabbard and throwing aside the louver doors. He lept for the strangely costumed, would-be destroyer. Nakashima was fast, and he hit the man at his waist, toppling him. But the man deflected his knife-blow to the side. He had not reckoned on the intruder's speed, agility—and strength.

The intruder rolled, and as Nakashima drove his knife down at the man's neck, a mighty hand stayed his effort. Had he but known he was attacking the Doomsday Warrior, the chauffeur would not have been so hasty.

Rockson spun to his feet and hit the defender with a head butt. But it was Nakashima's chance now to show his battle skills, and the hefty Japanese took the butt and twisted to the side, smashing his locked fists onto the back of Rockson's neck.

The Doomsday Warrior, seeing stars, nevertheless recovered and snapped into a crouch. He picked up his fallen oak staff and swung at Nakashima's knees. But the man jumped, and the blow swished through empty air.

Who the hell was this ferocious Japanese opponent, Rock wondered. But there was no time to speculate!

Nakashima again lunged with the big knife, and it was Rock's turn to be *gone!*

161

They faced off in a crouch, the Doomsday Warrior holding the club, the Japanese with the knife. Rockson didn't want to draw this out; any second now someone else could join the party.

Nakashima backed off toward a display case that held an ancient ball-and-chain mauler—a relic of the samurai knights. "I, Nakashima, diciple of Mastesr Killov, will destroy you," the Japanese servant yelled.

The glass case was shattered by his elbow, and quick as a flash, he picked up the chain weapon. Swinging it mightily in his left hand, he rushed to attack the intruder once more.

Rockson again rolled to the side and snapped back into a crouch. He grabbed his shotpistol but thought better of it! *No.* A sound like that given off by the pistol would rouse the whole damned tower. *He had to defeat this swarthy killman silently.*

Nakashima, his chain-and-iron-ball samurai weapon swinging with a *whoosh,* came at Rock again, intending to deliver the heavy spiked ball into his skull, then jab the knife into his gut for good measure.

Rockson lifted the oak staff suddenly, snagging the chain, and then, before Nakshima could let go of the chain end, Rock pulled the staff with all his might. The Japanese fell forward, and Rockson smashed the barrel of the shotpistol on his left temple.

There was a crack and a spurt of blood. Nakashima, his eyes rolling upward, fell like a lead-filled sack at Rocks' feet. And stayed down. Rock went over to him. Hesitantly, he felt for his pulse at his jugular and found no throb. He was dead, whoever he was.

Time to go back and smash the panel.

No. The panel could just be repaired. If Killov wasn't here to *die,* better to just plant the last of the listening devices. *Damn,* if he had realized he could actually get into Killov's lair, he'd have brought *plastique!* Especially since there were structural faults here because of the unsupported large south windows. He would return with explosives—sixty pounds would do. It would have to be placed one flight up, to put downward pressure on the window area; then *Goodbye tower!*

But to do that, he'd have to first cover up that he'd ever been here.

Rockson did a quick floor search and found no other occupants. Then, Rockson dragged the body to the window. He opened the window and lifted the dead man into the opening, and letting him roll out into empty air. He left the window open and glanced around quickly: broken glass, a few drops of blood—nothing a distraught man wouldn't commit if he was intending to *end it all by suicide.*

There was a loud thump outside—the body hitting. Well, it would have to *do,* Rock thought grimly. *Time to leave!*

Rock made his way down to the lobby via the same elevator. He managed to just get out the lobby door when a pair of KGB guards grabbed him. "What are you doing in a restricted area?" one asked. "Don't you see that bloody body lying there old man? Don't we have enough problems?"

"Excuse please!" Rock answered. "Winter sunset coats hills with—"

"Not so fast!" The guard that spoke grabbed him by his robe and said, "We've had about enough of you old silly poets roaming around the city at all hours. *Semenov!* Take this geriatric case to the looney bin! That will teach him to walk in a restricted area!"

Rock almost smiled. The jerkoff didn't realize he was holding onto the Doomsday Warrior! He let himself be led away—muttering poetry—into a police van. Surely, this was an opportune way to escape the immediate area!

CHAPTER 20

Being in the insane asylum was like being in hell. Rockson couldn't believe all this was happening to him. He had been injected with a strong drug the second he stepped out of the police van, just as he was about to dart away.

The first few hours were a dream, a hazy nightmare. All he remembered was being taken into the cell and again injected—this time with some drug that immediately made him feel paranoid, as if he were at the bottom of a deep pit, staring up at the menacing world above. Two hulking attendants had strapped him down on a dirty stretcher and wheeled him through long underground tunnels with steam rising out of pipes and past dark rooms that seemed to disappear into eternal blackness. He was taken to a small room with another patient already in it, a man who kept yelling something about the devil coming out of the sidewalk and eating all the Russians. I guess they put all the paranoid loonies in the same place, he thought, as he fell into unconsciousness.

When he awoke, two Japanese men in long white

coats walked in and introduced themselves. "Good morning, Mr. Noname. I am Dr. Nisai, and this is Dr. Hakamisha. We are here to help you."

"The only help you can give me," Rock said groggily, struggling against the straps that held him down, "is to get me out of here. I'm not insane—I'm the Doomsday Warrior!"

"Of course, of course. But first we would like to talk with you a little. Listen to what you say, too. Now, apparently you have been going around causing a lot of trouble for other people and yourself. Shouting some stupid old poetry at our Russian friends." The two doctors, one tall and thin, the other, short and nearly bald, stared at him. They smiled warm false smiles.

"Not stupid poems, you idiots," Rock yelled. "Basho!"

"Ah yes, Basho—the great," the tall one, Dr. Hakamisha said. "But why are you speaking English, Mr. Noname? Forgotten your Japanese?"

"I just can't believe that this is all happening. I thought it was just Russians that put people in mental hospitals for opposing them. I am a *friend* of the Japanese."

"Ah, a friend, Mr. Noname? What is a friend?"

Rock decided he had to risk it. He proceeded to tell them his story. About how he was part of an American attack team intent on destroying the tower's crystal weapon and Killov's occupying army. "Surely," he said, "you are *Japanese*. You are against Killov!"

When he had finished, the two doctors looked meaningfully at one another. Dr. Nisai—the short

166

bald one—took out a black notebook and said to Rock, "Mr. Noname, has it ever occurred to you that perhaps you are afraid of what the tower represents?"

"What the hell is that supposed to mean?" Rockson asked, moving uncomfortably within his bindings.

"Well the tower is large and stands erect. Very big. Tell me . . . do you feel *inferior* to it in any way? *Sexually* perhaps?"

Rock burst out laughing. "You mean you think I'm jealous of the potency of the Tokyo Tower? Well let me assure you, gentlemen, I've had no trouble in that department! Women have always found me completely satisfactory. In fact, I've been quite a ladies man in my day. Now let me go! I must destroy the crystal!"

The doctors looked happy. "Tell us about this, Mr.—Warrior?" Dr. Hakamisha said. "In great detail."

The questioning went on for almost an hour, then the two psychiatrists turned to leave.

"So now you know I'm all right. Right? Now let me out!"

"Oh yes, Mr. Noname," said Nisai. "All in due time. There's so much more to talk about." They both left, an amused sparkle in their beady eyes.

Rockson screamed, "Goddamn crazy bastards," as the two closed the door and locked it. He lurched and heaved against the bindings until his shoulders and arms were raw and red. The other patient in the room soon joined him, and the two men howled like wolves until a nurse came in and gave them each a shot of something. Rock suddenly felt very confused again.

167

And the other man, who had the bed behind his, started screaming again about the devil coming up through the sidewalk to eat the Reds.

Maybe he's right, Rock thought, dizzily. Maybe the devil *is* coming up through the sidewalks. Maybe they're right, these crazy docs. Or else—would I be shut up in a straight jacket just like this. I must really be crazy!

He laughed. That was it! It was just an hallucination. He really wasn't Ted Rockson; the Doomsday Warrior.

He didn't know who he was. He *was* Mr. Noname!

He slowly fell asleep, seeing dim forms that looked like mixtures of his doctors and the devil about his bed. They were rising from the sidewalks, flying right up through the concrete and high up into the sky. They circled the Tokyo Tower like vultures, drifting slowly, looking down on Mr. Noname, who ran like a frightened rabbit through the tunnels and dark basements of the mental hospital.

"Coming out of it now," a kindly female voice said. "My, what an unusual specimen. What did they say he was brought in for?"

"Shouting and being in a restricted area. He's Caucasian beneath the makeup. He must be a Russian gone mad," the Japanese doctor concluded.

Dr. Nisai scratched his bald pate, "Well, in that case—if he's not Japanese he will only be trouble! We'd better release him."

The grey-haired woman doctor started unsnapping

168

Rockson's straight jacket, but Hakashima grabbed her arm. "Don't do that! If he's Russian, we've already condemned ourselves to death for the way we've treated him so far! We must continue to list him as Mr. Noname and keep him here!"

The woman nodded. "I see your point."

They all left the room.

Rockson passed out again. When he awoke, he sat up. It was hard to do because he was still in a straight jacket. But his head felt clearer than it had since he arrived. He would have to use the time before he got another injection to try to escape. Or be here *forever.*

The other patient in the room—also in a straight jacket—spoke up.

"Ah, my weird friend," said the middle-aged, squat Japanese patient. "And just who might you be?" There was derision in his voice.

Rockson decided to tell the truth. If the truth confused the sane doctors, perhaps it would be clear to this insane man!

"I'm an American. I'm in town to destroy the Soviet weapon. Who are you?"

"Ah me? The name's Morimoto!"

Rock said, "Not The Morimoto, leader of the Bushido fighting clan?"

The man bowed his head. "Same as you state, my friend."

"You're just the man I'm looking for to help me," Rock said eagerly.

"Really?" Morimoto laughed. "Well, I think that

might be difficult. I can't help anyone in a straight jacket!"

Rock said, "I see what you mean . . . It looks grim. But a Freefighter never says die." Rock wished he believed what he had just said.

He explained why he had come. Rock told all, either because the mind drug was still working or an instinctive need prompted him to trust Morimoto.

"I will help you, sir," Morimoto said. "We *can* escape if you have some *ability*. And it is imperative that we get out of here within the hour!"

"Why?"

"They will drug us with the Q-14 formula—the one they use for long-term inmates. It makes you like a zombie. We must escape *now*. And as for *how*," Morimoto added, "I've been thinking of how for a month. All I needed was an accomplice. You have mismatched eyes, so you are undoubtedly a mutant. Are you double jointed, as most mutants are?"

"Somewhat—though it hurts like hell. I *can* disjoint my shoulders."

"Then, please remove yourself from your straight jacket by that method—then undo me."

"Then what?"

"There is a way out. If we can but be free of these damned jackets. Hurry!"

Rock grunted and groaned for five minutes. He then was out of the jacket, badly bruised and sore— but *out*.

"A regular Houdini," complimented Morimoto.

The Japanese was freed from his straight jacket by Rockson, and then Rock said, "Okay. Where's the

170

way out?"

"There," Morimoto said, pointing up at the top of the right wall. "That small opening. It's a grating."

"Too small to crawl through," Rock said, his heart sinking.

"Just *look* through the grate friend. What do you see?"

"It — is a room of some sort," Rock said, once up on the stretcher peering through the wire mesh grate.

"And on the wall are sets of levers. Do you see them?" Morimoto asked.

"Yes. There *are* levers," Rock replied.

"See the electrical wires at the baseboard in this room? What if we make a line-and-hook out of it and snag the lever marked cell three? That's the lever that opens our door. I learned that by observation on my trips to and from the electric-shock chamber."

"You're a whiz, Morimoto! But we need a good hook."

"There are several on our straight jackets!"

"Damned if you're not right, Morimoto, my pal. You're a genius!"

It took over an hour of careful throwing of the makeshift line and hook through the grating to snag the lever. Any second an attendant could have come in and discovered their work, but God, or the demigods that watch over fools, was on their side! Morimoto did the honors, jerking the line. The hook caught the lever and pulled it open before the hook fell.

Their cell's steel door slid open.

"After you," the Japanese said. "Just walk down that staircase over there. I've seen them take off their work smocks and put on their regular garments, and then they exit there."

They opened a wardrobe closet and found some doctor's jackets there, put them on and ran down the stairs. They were quickly out the street door into the steaming heat of the evening.

It was now time for Morimoto to ask questions. "Where do we go?"

Rock answered, "Anywhere! But fast!"

CHAPTER 21

Killov, who had returned just as they had been scraping his only friend off the sidewalk, spent the whole day in seclusion.

"Why, Nakashima, why?" he kept saying over and over. "Why did you commit suicide?"

Nakashima, Killov knew, was obsessed with death. Indeed, he had wanted to die—by Killov's hand. He had made the colonel promise to *personally* kill him. So why the suicide leap? Why couldn't he wait?

Killov grieved for himself, too. After all, he was alone again. No one except Nakashima had *ever* understood Killov. Understood that life is inherently evil, inherently bound up with the dark forces; understood that to live is to kill. Nakashima knew that every day man kills to survive. He knew that we eat the bodies of living things, we step on insects as we walk and we destroy their tiny homes when we build our homes. Nakashima knew and *appreciated* that life *was* killing. That life and death were inseparable. And the chauffeur knew that to truly live, you have to throw your will behind the forces of death.

Poor Nakashima—such a great person didn't deserve to die so ignominiously, he thought. And—there was something *fishy* about his death. Killov, for that reason, had ordered the first men upon the scene be sent to his office.

The officer who had first found the body, the one who had given the report of the Japanese madman being at the scene instants after Nakashima fell, now was sent in. Killov looked up at the nervous corporal's pock-marked face.

"Kimlovsky," Killov shouted, "what happened to that madman you found at the scene? Who was he? Did you let him escape?"

"Sir! He was not let go. I sent him to the insane asylum, sir!"

"Really?" Killov said. "That was—insufficient. He should have been held for questioning by me. I suspect that he had something to do with Nakashima's fall. I *sense* it!" Adrenaline flowed like an icy river of energy into Killov's rapidly beating heart. "Quickly—get on the phone to the asylum! Tell them to make sure to hold the man you sent to them for my interrogation."

Kimlovsky made a hasty scramble to the phone on the boomerang-shaped desk and got the asylum on the line. Killov saw the officer jerk upright and nearly yank the handphone off its wire when he heard what the person on the line said.

Killov rushed over and said, "What? What is it Kimlovsky?"

Kimlovsky's face was drained of blood. He man-

174

aged to stutter out, "H-he—the prisoner has escaped!"

Killov wrenched the phone from Kimlovsky's trembling hand. "I will deal with *you* later."

"Attention," he snarled into the receiver. "This is Killov. What did the escaped man look like?"

"Why—quite Caucasian," the Japanese doctor on the line said. "Perhaps he was a mutant. He had mismatched light- and dark-blue eyes. . . ."

"Rockson! Rockson is here!" Killov gasped, dropping the receiver. It all started falling into place: That other strange event—the destruction of the Pleasure Pagoda! Just like Rockson—rescuing prostitutes!

"Rockson must be the one that killed my only friend!" Killov raged. *"Rockson."*

Morimoto and Rockson were at that very moment breaking open the door of a 340X Toyota racing car in the KGB parking lot two blocks south of the asylum. The ignition system, Rock was happy to find out, was the key type. Just a little hot wiring under the dashboard, and the big engine roared to life. The low-slung, wide-tired, red car screeched out of the lot and into the main thoroughfare of New Tokyo, Rockson at the wheel.

A guard ran alongside the car and grabbed the windowsill. Rock found the automatic window control and pushed it, quickly raising the window on the man's fingers. With a howl of pain, the guard fell away—minus a few fingernails.

The whole city was full of traffic. They were soon

immersed in the mass of cars. The 340X was a four star general's personal sports car. Aside from its speed, it had one other bonus — an R.P.G. was lying right there on the back seat! Rock drove slowly, hoping to get across the city and onto the swamp road without being spotted.

All was well until the general that *owned* the car happened to be in a jeep rushing back to the lot to get his sports car. When he saw it rush by him, he yelled the Russian equivalent of "Shit, that's my wheels!" From that moment on, it was to be a wild shoot-em-up chase. The kind of action Rockson revelled in!

"Hold tight," he yelled, and bounced the low-slung model onto the sidewalk, scattering shoppers in front of the Takamaya Department Store. He saw the jeep and the glint of a pair of .45s — or the Red equivalent — bound into his rearview mirror. Then there was a series of pops.

"Down," Rock exclaimed, as the rear window shattered and bullets whizzed by to duplicate the damage on the windshield. He twisted the wheel, and the car rolled into the street again. He roared through a red light, sending other cars careening to avoid him. "Get that R.P.G. up Morimoto. You know how to fire it?"

"Can do," the Japanese said, lifting the grenade shooter and shouldering it. "It's loaded!"

"Well — let 'em have it; I have my hands full."

As the sports car bobbed and weaved, Morimoto sighted through the broken rear window. Finally, he pulled the trigger. Their ears popped, and the car filled with smoke, forcing Rock to brake to a halt.

But the occupants of the pursuing jeep fared worse. The shell scored a direct hit, blasting them to incendiary bits, which rained down blood.

Rockson, hearing sirens everywhere, turned a half dozen corners, roared through an underground garage, cut down yet another sidewalk, and then spun the smoking 340X onto a quiet side street. He slowed down and made a good guess which way to go. Shortly, they reached the vicinity of the home of Chimura. Rock said, "It's just across that swampy area. Can you see the house over the reeds?"

"Yes," Morimoto replied, "we leave the car here?"

"Yes—get out. I'm ditching it."

Rock started the car backward to the other side of the road, at the same time he clicked the driver's side door open. Taking careful aim, he put the pedal to the floor. At the instant the car leapt from the road toward the reeds, he leapt out and rolled. The vehicle touched the top of the nearest cattails, then fell splashing into the reeds. A flock of birds took wing, startled. The sports car slowly sank until there was hardly a trace of its passing.

"Well, that's *that,*" Rock said. "Come on—"

They waded through the shallower part of the swamp, and then climbed up the embankment to the bamboo walls of the compound. They went through the open gate and came to the door.

"Wipe your feet," Rock said, and knocked.

Killov, as the search for Ted Rockson expanded throughout the city, stood silently by the sheet-covered body lying in the middle of his office floor. Everyone he had ordered to be there was silent; no one dared to even clear his throat. The KGB colonel finally lifted his lowered head, turned to Major Bukrov, officer in charge of the funeral, and said softly, "Summon the best surgeon we have—and some of his assistants. Have him suture up Nakashima's wounds; make my friend look nice. Have the body cleaned off. I don't want blood. After that, wrap the body in a gold sheet and return it to my suite. I will make further preparations. Have the body sent back in half an hour!"

The officer blurted, "B-but he's dead. Why suture him?"

Killov's eyes narrowed. "I *command,* and you *don't* question!"

Killov was truly mad, the officer realized, but he still had to be obeyed. He saluted, and he and the five other KGB pallbearers started to lift the body.

Killov turned to the window. Once the door closed, he lifted a handkerchief to his eyes for a quick moment, dabbing away two tiny droplets. Tears! What was happening to him? Never had Killov wept for any man—until now!

He replaced the handkerchief in his pocket and sat down to wait, brooding behind his black marble desk.

Exactly a half hour later, the silver elevator opened, and Nakashima's body was wheeled back into the suite on a roll table. As ordered, the body had been sutured and placed under a golden cloth.

The colonel went to the golden sheet and pulled it back. He smiled, for the surgeons had done a good job. Killov bent and kissed Nakashima's still-soft cheek. As he did so, he whispered, "I will now do as I promised you."

Killov stood back and held out his arm. "Romanov, bring me the seventeenth-century sword from the trophy room." Shortly the jackbooted KGB officer, who had gone to fetch the sword, returned. He goose stepped forward and held the samurai sword out. Killov solemnly took it from him and turned to the body and raised the sword. "As I promised you . . ." Killov said, almost inaudibly.

As the other "mourners" stood in aghast wonder, Killov swung the blade down violently and lopped the dead man's head off!

Nakashima's head rolled on the floor.

Killov, mumbling what sounded like a lullabye, picked the bloody head up by the hair. Cradling it in his arms, he put it back on the table, on the body's chest. Then Killov himself wheeled the stretcher to the center of the room, to a position right in front of his desk.

The metal plate located in the floor in front of Killov's desk had been perplexing to the officers, and they had noted a similar plate above it on the ceiling. They had all surmised it was a metal detector of some sort, something that showed Killov if the person before him had hidden weapons.

But it was *not* a metal detector—it was an execution device, one of the many ways the colonel guarded himself against would-be assassins!

"Stand back, if you value your lives," Killov intoned to the six pallbearers. He took the seat at his desk and said, "Now for the cremation." He flipped the far right switch located on his intercom unit.

Huge bolts of electricity suddenly coursed between the floor and ceiling metal plates and through the gold-swathed body of Nakashima. Soon the gold sheet and then the body and head burst into a fiery incandescence. The heat, fed pure oxygen by hidden fans in the floor, turned the area before the desk into a convection-microwave oven, quickly incinerating the body and the stretcher. Soon all that was left was a small bubbling mass of motley cromium and some white-glowing dust.

The pallbearers had backed off until they had banged against the wall. They had never expected *this* sort of madness, even from the leader they *knew* was demented.

Killov said, switching off the killing device, "When it cools off, remove the remains on the floor and place Nakashima's ashes in that vase." He pointed to an ancient green urn—an early Chin dynasty vase sitting on a table in the corner.

No one said a single word. It would be done.

Rockson sat with Morimoto in the cavern speaking to all the Freefighters, explaining the events that lead up to Morimoto and himself returning to Chimura's house. Chen then reported that he had monitored the bugs Rockson had planted in the tower and found out that Killov would have the crystal weapon operational at midnight *that very night!*

"Then," said Rock emphatically, "we act now to prevent its use! Morimoto—we'll need your Bushido swordsmen."

Morimoto set down his tea cup and bowed slightly. "I will go and summon my men, Rockson."

"How? The KGB troops are in a state of maximum alert. The streets are—"

Morimoto said, "They will be looking for you, not a short Japanese man with a peasant's garb. I will meet you in an hour—back here—with the best men I can gather! This will be an excellent place to launch our attack from."

Togamatsu, an utterly bald, thin man of sixty years of age, squatted on a polished wood floor with a group of students clustered in a semi-circle around him. Togamatsu was putting the last spiral twist on the third "astral" twig in his flower arrangement. It had taken ten hours to reach this point in the spiritually fulfilling process. During all of the time, his seven disciples watched Togamatsu work with intense rapture.

Ikebana, the sacred art of flower arrangement, was very ancient. No one knew when it had begun—perhaps in prehistoric times, with the Ainu mystics. *Ikebana* was known in its present form—and unadulterated—since the 8th century when it was practiced in the Imperial Court by a Flower General. The arrangements of the flowers were difficult and exacting, inspired by aesthetic and philosophical principles

181

of several *dojos,* or schools. In Togamatsu's lineage — the Ikenobo school dating from the fourteenth century — the prime object of the design meditation was to symbolize in the arrangement of the flowers and twigs by the *law of TEN CHI JIN.* This was the arrangement of heaven: the firmament on top, the earth at its foot and man in between.

But now, a gentle knock came on the door. Heads turned. Togamatsu withdrew his scissors. "Come in."

The doorknob turned. The students held their breath. The teacher had interrupted his long work. Was the knock at the door some spirit?

"Morimoto-san." The teacher smiled and bowed. "Many thought you dead."

The students put their heads down to the floor. Such an honor it was to see Morimoto, the man who mastered *all* the seven meditative and martial arts of indescribable beauty — *Ikebana* being one of them — was here.

"How is it that a man we thought dead yet lives?"

"Later, Togamatsu-san! I come with news — the time has come! We rise in revolt! We Bushido have now been unleashed by the council!"

Togamatsu said, "It is good," and went to his sacred wooden chest. The students filed out of the room. This was something only another Bushido *Master* could witness. Togamatsu lifted the lid and took out a magnificent sword. He bowed to his family's shrine and put the sword over the flickering candles before his grandfather's picture. "This sword, which was owned by our fallen great great grandfather who died in battle at Okinawa, I rededicate to the emperor of death! It has been carried by each successive senior male member of the Togamatsu clan in honor. *Let me be so worthy!*"

With that, Togamatsu put the sword in a scabbard and, standing, attached the belt-linked scabbard to his waist. The movements caused a wavering in the incense smoke. He smiled at Morimoto. "The ancestors are happy."

Together with the seven — now armed — students, Togamatsu left with Morimoto to rouse the other Bushido.

Morimoto and Togamatsu appeared at the home of the *Sumie-e* watercolor painter Geiden and summoned him in mid-brushstroke. He too rushed to a sacred chest and put on a war outfit of chain mail. With reverence to his ancestors and their shrine, he took up his ancient samurai sword. He added twelve more stout lads.

Then the three masters roused the ceramic potter Ahurmaki, who was decorating a jade urn. "Come," Morimoto implored, "we fill many funeral urns today!"

Then they went to the Zepanai theater, interrupting, a *Noh-play,* a days-long performance of spiritual significance — one that was, fortunately, concluding.

Though he had acted for the last twelve hours straight, the lead actor, Fukamura said, "I am not tired in the face of enemies. *Always ready,* that is my family's motto!" He too gathered his students. The group moved on through the darkened alley, separately, and reconvened at Harumotu's house.

He was asleep, but there was his most magnificent

woodcut ever. Harumotu was over sixty years old —
like the other venerable Bushido men — but age only
sharpens the sword and skill of a Bushido master!
Harumotu was roused, and the master was quickly
informed of the situation.

He dressed and took one look back at his woodcut — the female form of his late wife in her early years
perfectly rendered in a carving. She was surrounded in
the woodcut by carefully rendered waves with foaming edges. The whole sense of the woodcut was that of
"leading one into infinity — through death." There was
a poem chiseled down one edge of the work. "Life a
one-day blossom."

"Your finest work," said Morimoto. "Worthy of
Hirshige-san himself!"

Without false modesty, for the statement was obviously *true,* Harumotu said, "Yes it is fine — and I am
glad, for we now go to battle. I will join my wife and
the ancestors' honored urns in the temple, a happy,
completed artist!"

The rest of the Bushido swordsmen were then
quickly rounded up.

The gathered Bushido, who had taken separate
routes, all ended in the reed field near Chimura's
compound. They came together and marched forward
down the gravel road along the brook's bank. Each
was dressed in his family's traditional battle gear, each
man carried a sprig of spring flower and two weapons: one, the heavy *katama,* a two-handed weapon,
sharply pointed, with an edge as keen as that of a

razor; the other weapon was the short ritual knife for in-fighting — or for *hari-kari* — depending on success or failure!

Rockson was glad indeed to see these forty-seven formidable fighters join his attack force!

CHAPTER 22

Killov looked at the three technicians on either side of his emaciated frame at the weapon-control panel. "A few adjustments," he muttered, turning two dials. *"There* — all set! Ready!"

One by one the technicians called out, "Ready!"

This was it! Killov, trembling with anticipation, touched the master ON switch lovingly, savoring the *click*. The crystal weapon was operational!

But . . . why did he feel that something could YET go wrong? He had drawn an impenetrable perimeter of steel around the tower; but Rockson was still at large, and that man was *uncanny* at penetrating defenses!

Killov pushed the thought away.

He turned the master power switch to the FULL POWER position. The pulsing hum of the crystal, absorbing ten megawatts of electricity on the tower above them, shook the room.

"Now . . ." Killov snapped to ON position the ten levers marked SAT CON." He was now linked up to the space satellite mirror. The space satellite hadn't been activated in over one hundred years, but that was no problem; the vacuum of space preserved it all perfectly. This was the crucial moment. Would the huge, collapsed mirror begin its twenty-minute-long expansion? Would it fan out to its full width and respond to the telemetry instructions from the ground? Was the code book Killov had found on Johnston Island accurate?

Holding his breath, he punched in the code.

Bulbs lit up; circuits snapped into place. The great mirror twenty-three thousand miles above them, in the silence of space, was responding to his message! It worked!

The data pouring forth on the screens before the colonel indicated that indeed the mirror would deploy! Killov turned to the technical assistant next to him and said, "Success!"

The man smiled nervously. "C-Congratulations, Colonel." His future was supposedly assured; he had helped Killov get ultimate power over the whole world, but the technician still feared Killov.

The colonel sat back and proudly observed the dozens of meters and screens that told the story. The crystal was nearly at full power, a day ahead of schedule. Rockson had come, but he was *too late!*

Never had the KGB leader felt so *elated.* Always before, Rockson had destroyed his carefully planned enterprise at the last moment—but not now.

Ah, the sheer exultation of *finally* defeating the penultimate American. Nakashima had made the event possible. He had died to save the project, died to save his master's greatest work!

Oh, Nakashima, Killov thought. I shall build a monument to you in this capital; you shall be revered even above the forty-seven Ronin for your loyalty.

"I will now assume visual control," Killov told the technicians.

Killov's seat now started to rise from the floor, and simultaneously, a circular orifice began to dilate open in the ceiling. He would actually fire the crystal weapon from his personal survival sphere. After he had studied the data on the crystal, he had feared that severe injury might result from the high-pitched sound emitted by the weapon when it was used. So he had this steel-alloy ball created. He would have its added sound protection when he let the havoc loose.

The technicians? — Why, they had lived long enough to complete their work!

Killov rose like an ascending angel of death until he was encased in the black sphere. Then the floor was closed beneath his chair.

There was nothing but darkness. Slowly, the stars came out. They weren't real stars; this sphere was a planetarium, too, as well as the weapon-control globe. The projector was designed to give Killov a perspective from space as if he were actually in high orbit, at the position of the death-ray mirror that would bounce the crystal's beam back to earth, destroying whatever target Killov aimed it at via his chair's targeting controls.

Killov twisted the seat slightly so he could peer down at the perfect holographic representation of planet Earth. It looked so *real:* blue oceans, twists of clouds, brown continents. He was almost dizzy. He steadied himself; still it was hard not to gasp for air. It was hard not to believe he was *not* in airless space! But breath came easily in the cool air-conditioned sanctuary.

"Now," he said aloud, and lifted his right hand over the controls of the chair arm. He selected a point of view ten miles from the space mirror. Instantly the stars winked and changed. He beheld the dangerous-looking, serrated-edged laser-focusing mirror floating in space.

Fully extended.

Good.

Next, Killov projected a section of western Siberia before him. He expanded the view until he saw the Soviet city of Vladivostock clearly. He smiled. Soon it would be ashes—as a demonstration to Premier Vassily of Killov's ultimate powers!

His left hand directed the power-surging crystal's alignment. He set it at an angle on its rotary base, so that it was 45 degrees tilted to the west. A red light came on, and a control beeped. Targeting of the city in Siberia was now accomplished.

Killov began to activate his worldwide, radio-interruption signal. Everywhere there were radios or televisions, the local broadcast would turn to static. Then the populace would hear his booming voice, hear his *commands* alone! Killov cleared his throat and threw the switch.

"People on Earth, this is Killov!" He smiled. He liked that line. It sounded like a science-fiction movie!

"Surrender to me and my KGB forces or see the destruction of your cities! You will now witness a sample of my destructive capability!" Killov didn't specify where he would strike because he knew it could take some practice to correctly aim the shots.

"All leaders—after my demonstration of power, you have fifteen minutes to surrender!"

Killov gave the frequency for their surrender. Then he fired the weapon.

Even in his steel-alloy survival ball, Killov's rat-colored hair stood on its end. The ground-effect of the weapon was stronger than he'd expected.

Below the colonel, the technicians screamed and held their ears as blood burst from their eyes and trickles from their noses. Their fingers smoked, and they quivered and convulsed, sliding from their seats onto the floor. Windows burst all around the city as the red lazer beam from the crystal atop the tower shot out into the sky. It sounded like a hundred jets had broken the sound barrier simultaneously.

Because Killov had no assistance from his—now dead—technicians below, his shot missed its target. Instead of devastating Vladivostock, the lazer beam bounced off target from the space mirror and headed for the Pacific Ocean off the Siberian coast.

Admiral Mintchov limped back and forth along the bridge deck of the Soviet aircraft carrier *Vostok*. Why did he feel so apprehensive? His fleet's exercises off the Phillipines had gone off without a hitch. Ashore, he would receive more medals, more honors. Already — at the age of twenty-eight — he was the youngest, most decorated admiral in the Soviet fleet! But that was happenstance. He *happened* to be in Washington, D.C., as a lieutenant, two years ago during the premier's summit meeting there, when Killov had attacked from nowhere. Mintchov, donning frog-man gear, had helped Rahallah, the premier's aide, rescue Vassily from the clutches of the mad colonel, assuring Mintchov's future. He was injured in the rescue, losing an arm, a leg and one eye in the hellfire from Killov's troops. But Mintchov was not so injured that he didn't enjoy his ascendancy to high command. Yet today he was apprehensive.

He opened the main door and went out on the deck. There was a feeling of strange *warmth* in the air. He looked up at the sky, and Mintchov's jaw dropped! The clouds were spreading out like a smoke ring from some unseen center. The air in the center of the halo of white was darkening — no, turning red. And growing brighter.

"Oh my God . . ." Mintchov muttered.

A blinding red funnel descended from the hollow spot in the sky. A searing hot wind tore across the fleet from the swirling funnel. The calm waters were now rising in a tidal wave of steaming death.

Mintchov saw a destroyer capsize, its sailors falling, white uniforms ablaze, off its red molten decks as it rolled over. Then Mintchov screamed, for his clothes and skin burst into white-hot flames. The scream was short-lived.

The close-up telescopic projection of the HIT area showed a twenty-mile-wide steam cloud over a boiling wave-tossed hell.

Killov was not satisfied. He corrected for his angle error and fired the death beam again. He again felt the power surge as his hair crinkled and stood straight up, its dead-mouse color changing to electric blue. He foamed at the mouth and laughed madly as Hangchow, China evaporated. He was insulated here in his shell, but half the city below must be screaming in agony at the ultrasonic boom of the crystal being fired above their heads! *Let the bastards die—decrease the surface population.*

He tried to re-adjust and hit Siberia—anywhere in Siberia. "Let's see," he mumbled, totally absorbed. "I was six hundred miles to the left, a two degree correction. . . ."

Satisfied at the slight shift of the space mirror, Killov again tried to hit Vladivostock.

The Zero-Impulse Laser Crystal Holograph—the ZILCH—was true to its mark this time. In Vladivostock, 160,000 people were going about their chores. They of course had heard Killov's radio broadcast, but the people of Vladivostock hadn't really had time to think about what it meant. They had either kept doing what they were doing or stood in small clusters in the snow-piled streets, speculating about what exactly the meaning of the message was for them.

In a few seconds they all found out: The sky broiled black then red, and to a howling high-pitched whistle, it *opened up.*

A red lazer funnel descended and everything—

houses, cars, buildings, men, women, children—burst into flames where they stood. An incinerator wind fanned the flames until all was *ash*.

In a few minutes the city was just smoke and howling steam—and the echos of 160,000 screams on the fetid wind.

"Well, *that's better,*" Killov said, observing the red pimple as it appeared on the Siberian steppes of the projected Earth.

He switched on the radio-interrupt frequency again.

"Ten minutes to surrender, Vassily," Killov boomed out. He clicked the radio off. That took care of Russia!

Killov immediately started to manipulate controls, re-aligning the crystal and the space mirror.

It was time to DO America!

CHAPTER 23

The Freefighters, the Polynesian warriors and Morimoto's many Bushido fighters advanced through the Tokyo streets. Bloody citizens were staggering through fields of broken glass, screaming; cars were crashing as the crystal fired again. The sky was an ominous yellow. Rock saw the second deadly lazer beam leap from atop the tower and was nearly thrown off his feet by the concussion of the shot.

Rock hoped that the beam wasn't aimed toward the Rockies! His ears hurt, but they hadn't burst. He could thank Chen for that! Chen had thought of the attack force's need for earplugs.

The plan was to divide into four squads: one led by Rockson, the other squads led by Chen, Scheransky and Detroit Green.

The whole group now had reached the downtown area. At the corner of Hibiya-Dori Avenue and Sotobori, Rock signaled with a wave of his hand for the squads to split off. He continued sprinting down Hibiya-Dori with Archer and McCaughlin and fifteen of the Bushido. Rock was amazed that the old Morimoto not only kept up but didn't even appear winded

The populace—those that were still standing after the concussions from the tower—cheered and waved them on, yelling *"Banzai, Banzai!"* The people had grown to hate Killov and the KGB. Rock appreciated the encouragement, but he hoped they'd keep the hell out of the way and leave the assault to his professionals!

Rockson put his Liberator up in the air at a downtown intersection. They were just 100 yards from the south leg of the immense tower.

"This is it," he shouted. "Get your weapons ready."

He checked his watch, then waited twelve seconds. "The other units should be in position," he yelled, "so let's GO!"

They poured around a building into the square. Instantly, artillery at the Eiffel-like tower started hurtling howitzer shells at them. Two Bushido were blasted to bits of flesh and blood as they ran.

"Behind the vehicles," Rockson commanded. "McCaughlin, do you have those grenades?"

"I got 'em!" Before Rock could say anything, the tow-headed Freefighter was sprinting in a zig-zag, as the emplacement tracer bullets from KGB machine guns were dogging his steps, inches behind. As McCaughlin ran, he snapped out two pineapples—heavy fragmentation grenades—from his bandolier. In a double-throw that Rockson never saw him try before, he hurtled them toward the sandbag howitzer emplacement. Then, his momentum carrying him forward, McCaughlin rolled and dove toward shelter behind the burning wreck of a Mazda sedan.

Both of McCaughlin's grenades hit dead on target. Reds flew up into the air, the bastards sailing like naughty kids on a super-trampoline of death.

But it was not over by a long shot. Though the big guns fell silent, a squad of KGB came running out of the south-tower-leg's fortifications. They were met by withering fire from the Freefighter's Liberators.

Rock couldn't divert any of his men to help the other groups, for they were staring down the gun barrel of fifty KGB killers.

The KGB opened fire in return as the attackers spread out and continued to fire from cover. The Bushido were using ancient large-barrelled, single-shot pistols from the Meiji Era. Amazingly, they were taking out as many KGB as the Freefighter's Liberator SMGs.

As the remaining KGB broke and ran, the Bushido lept forward and caught up with them, slashing them down like wheat at harvest time in hell. The Bushido, at the same time, dodged sniper fire.

"God, we could use fifty of 'em," McCaughlin yelled.

"Stop shouting and start shooting!" Rock spat back, slamming another full clip in his Liberator's hot breech. With the big SMG on his hip, he stood up, firing a waist-high series of bursts. The explosives bullets cut the numbers of KGBers in half.

But there were Soviet troops on all sides now — coming out of *holes*. The Freefighters were encircled, in the open.

A steel rattrap!

Crossfire raked the area; two of the brave Bushido

fell, jerking like bewitched dolls.

This isn't working, Rockson thought, as he ejected a spent magazine and slammed another from his belt pack into place. Just in time, he opened up on two KGBers who had gotten just twenty feet away. They stumbled forward, their stomachs afire from the explosive bullets' heat, and collapsed at his feet.

Seeing no other shelter from the rain of bullets except their bodies, he dropped behind them. The KGBers carcasses were still gurgling blood. Rock emptied his rifle once more, then he took up the Kalashnikov one of the dead soldiers had dropped.

The Russian weapon was the equal of the Liberator and had a bigger clip, half expended. Shots were flying everywhere. The only good thing about the cross fire, Rock thought, was that many of the Reds were being shot down by their own side.

But the Sovs had the numbers; they could afford losses. Rockson's group was being whittled down bit by bit.

Rock was amazed to see Archer suddenly walk right out into the open. The bearded near-mute's leather hat blew off — or was shot away — but he didn't flinch. Was Archer *mad?*

"Archer," Rock yelled, "get the hell *down!"*

No reply. The mountain man was headed toward the tower entrance and drawing more and more fire. Had he snapped? Rockson tried to pick off some of the shooters peppering Archer, who didn't even wince as bullets pinged all around him.

The maze of small quartz crystals buried in Archer's head—ever since a life-saving operation to repair a battle wound—started *glowing*.

Archer's tiny head crystals suddenly took in a bright blue, waving line of electrical discharge *coming from the tower*.

Leilani was huddled down behind a turned-over Toyota Camry near to Rockson. He crawled over to her and put her helmet back on her head; the helmet had come off. She had that odd far-off look in her eyes. *"Leilani*—what's happening to Archer—do you know?"

"Crystal . . . help . . . him . . . now," she said softly." Crystal . . . is . . . powering Archer. Through his head crystal. The Gnaa crystal is . . . protecting him. So we can come . . . and destroy it."

"It *wants* to die?"

"It's in pain . . . oh such *pain!*" A tear edged down from each of her doe-eyes. "It helps us—through Archer."

"So *that's* it," Rock exclaimed. "Well—we can use the crystal's help in this battle. How long will it power Archer?"

"Few . . . more . . . minutes. . . ."

Rock looked up and saw that the red, yellow and blue lines of force were feeding from the giant crystal weapon into Archer.

The Doomsday Warrior saw Archer lift up the rear bumper of an abandoned truck and twist his arms. The bumper bent and tore off the truck. The mountain man, grinning from ear to ear, walked toward a group of advancing KGB troops, ignoring their fire.

He swished the bumper back and forth, knocking the troops down. They fell like tenpins, still holding their smoking SMGs, with astonished looks on their faces.

Archer had been hit a hundred times, and yet he lived! He picked up one of the spilled-soldier's weapons. He raised the Kalashnikov to fire point-blank at another Red that roled from behind a charred truck to the right. The new opponent levelled his big-barrelled SMG at Archer. The burst of .50 calibre slugs hit the near-mute square in his fat gut, *but with no results*. Archer's return fire threw the KGBer's body back like a loosely stuffed scarecrow of death.

Rock looked around and saw Killov's troops abandoning their posts, fleeing Archer. The Freefighters were in a position to take the south leg of the tower and use its big guns to take out the other fortifications.

He saw a group of Surfcombers fling their power-tridents at a pair of KGBers. The Russians fell, spurting blood around the huge tines of the long forks. Polynesian paddle-bludgeons cracked heads right and left in close combat. Bullets howled.

Archer's superman-act had turned the tide of battle.

Rock took up his binocs and scanned the other tower legs. He saw that Chen's group was pinned down and taking heavy fire. Rockson had the option of either helping Chen's beleaguered attack team, or advancing his own whittled-down force toward the tower building. A tough choice. But if he could add

Chen's group to his own *before* advancing on the building . . .

Rock glanced over at his strange mountain man friend. His head was still sparking with electrical discharges from the strange linkup with the tower crystal.

"Archer," he ordered, "come on—let's help Chen!"

Archer dropped the KGBer he was throttling and waved. "Okay!"

Somewhere up in the tower, a large calibre machine gun started raking the vicinity with explosive rounds. But the KGB bastards had trouble seeing because of the oil smoke, or else didn't care. They hit several of their own men.

"Advance on the west tower leg," Rock ordered his troops.

Taking advantage of the smoke conditions, the sprinting forces, with Archer in the lead, got behind the Reds on their left flank. Tridents flew again, Bushido cut down the dodging Reds. But Rock saw a tank coming into the square—*Damn, where the hell did they get that?*

Archer turned to the tank, said something like "MEE GET!" and walked toward it, his head still sparking and trailing red, white and blue electrical discharges.

"Archer, *don't—* " Rock shouted. But either the giant didn't hear or didn't obey. He and the tank were racing at one another like two mad bulls in a farmer's field.

Only one would survive—and how could a human best a tank?

Yet, as they collided, it was the tank that lost and burst into smoke and then flames. Archer obviously had some sort of force field protecting him — a gift of the crystal. Cheering wildly, the Freefighter groups merged.

Rock saw Chen bounding rather gracelessly atop a Dasun X-7. What the hell was he holding? And what did he carry on his back?

Rockson soon found out. The Chinese-American let loose a sweeping hellfire of liquid napalm from his commandeered flamethrower, into the steel-rim holes dotted around the area.

Screaming, burning Russians rose up from their hidden positions and scurried helter-skelter. They were either cut down by their startled comrades or collapsed of their own volition. Other fighters, draining gasoline tanks, ignited other hidden rats. In the confusion of burning screaming runners, Rockson ran right at a machine-gun pillbox and dove in. He plunged his dagger into the nearest uniformed shape and, finding one other soldier still alive in the emplacement, twisted the blade out of the first body and stuck it deep into the second man's windpipe.

There was a tripod-mounted .105 in the bastion. He took up the big gun and sighted down the hot barrel. Shells fed down the belt into his new sewing machine of death. Rock stitched out a fabric of destruction on the KGBers he sighted.

The Freefighters and their allies were winning now. And just in time, for Archer's head suddenly stopped dancing with crystal power. The giant stood in the open, his skull top smoking slightly, a bedazed expres-

202

sion on his face.

"Archer, come over here—you're not invincible anymore!"

The near-mute nodded slightly and walked slowly, like a zombie in thick mud, over to Rockson. The Doomsday Warrior pulled his friend down beside him behind the sandbag barrier wall and said, "Good work, Arch!"

"WHAAT HAPPEN?" Archer said, confused.

"You're a hero! We're winning, thanks to you."

Now it was time to advance on the central building itself.

"Attack," Rock shouted as he jumped up on top of a smoking, metal tank part. He waved his men onward, and then joined the run forward himself. The other victorious attack squads also advanced on the run toward the tower building's steel-shuttered doors.

Killov's steel trap was now just history.

"Detroit get the KGB positions at the door with your grenades. Morimoto! Get that contingent by the side with your men," the Doomsday Warrior ordered.

As Rock led his four surviving Polynesian warriors forward around the KGB positions on the right flank, Detroit took out his grenades. Jumping on an abandoned jeep's hood, he tossed the fused pineapples accurately at the six-inch-wide gun slits in the steel-shuttered lobby doors.

The two grenades went through the openings one after the other. There was a two second pause, then the steel doors blew outward, bits of flesh and bone among the shreds of metal shielding.

"Good work, Detroit," Rock yelled. "Men—advance. The building is ours!"

That was not *quite* true. But it's best, Rock thought, to be optimistic!

CHAPTER 24

Killov, cut off from the sounds of the desperate battle below by the steel-alloy walls of his control sphere, aimed a last "demonstration" shot. This one was toward Baltimore, Maryland. He had just positioned the crystal and space mirror to perfection and was about to pull the trigger when an annoying beep-beep-beep started on the control chair's left arm.

"Damn," he cursed as the sudden noise made his arm jerk. His aim was sent way off as he hit the destruct button. He burned a hundred miles of the Caribbean Sea off the coast of Cuba, instead of his target.

Killov realized that the beeping noise was from the built-in red emergency phone on the chair's arm.

Was there an emergency? He supposed that his troops were being engaged by some ragtag enemy. He had long expected the sullen natives to erupt in futile opposition to his rule. Well, his officers could handle it — at least for another five minutes. He had important things to accomplish — a whole world to bring to utter prostration, millions to incinerate. What could be more important?

Angrily Killov cut the sound switch on the phone without picking up. *Nothing* must interfere with his work!

Seventy-two stories below Killov's insulated domain, his burly KGB chief, Igor Stepanovitch, let the telephone receiver dangle and started firing his Kalashnikov on full automatic. The strange intruders — a band of old Japanese men with swords, tall khaki-clad Caucasians, and near-naked South Sea islanders — had breached the security doors of the lobby and killed half the KGB force defending it. His clip jammed, and he ejected it, sliding another into his weapon. Now the intruders were pouring at him with blood in their eyes. He ducked bullets that clipped the marble wall where his head had just been. Stepanovitch pulled up his big SMG and let rip, smiling as two of the Japanese storybook swordsmen fell. But no — they hadn't been hit, they had merely rolled out of his fire. Before he could reload again, Igor Stepanovitch felt a sudden sharp sting on his neck, then the world was swirling, whirling.

Why? Why was the world whirling?

As the roar in his ears rose, a red circle of gathering darkness was closing in on his vision, and he found out why the world had been whirling. Stepanovitch saw his own headless body crumpling to the ground. The KGB officer realized that he was now just a severed head, and he started to scream. Only a voiceless gasp came out. He was seeing the things of this

206

sad globe for the last time, from bursting eyes in his bodyless head!

Fade to BLACK.

Morimoto wiped the sword blade on the headless corpse's uniform jacket. To avoid the fire from another guard's position, he again dove for cover behind a garbage dumpster. Blood trickled from a hit in his thigh.

Rockson, meanwhile, rushed for the silver elevator with a sixty-pound pack of high explosives over his shoulder. Chen and McCaughlin covered him as he bounded over spilled bodies and made it into the elevator area.

Two KGBers came running right at Rockson, with fixed bayonets. The Soviets were caught with the whooshing steel edges of Chen's star darts. Their deaths were instantaneous as the blades dug into their bodies and exploded.

There was too much action going on for praise, but Rock yelled out a brief "Good work!" to the Freefighter. "Get to the other end of the lobby and secure it: I'm going to head upstairs on the elevator."

Rock had a simple plan—pick the lock again and ride the thing up. One flight past the madman's suite, just under the tower roof, he would plant the explosives.

Ignoring the firefight raging all around, and the spatter of bullets that ricocheted around the lobby, Rock started to work, putting the heavy bomb satchel down for a moment on the marble floor. But he was not allowed a moment. . . .

Careening around a corner swept a pair of ancient-looking nemesis. Not Russians — something worse!

Rockson now faced off against two Japanese samurai — two of the disgraced samurai's, no doubt, that had thrown in their lot with Killov.

The keen-eyed thick-set men were naked to the waist. They drew their swords and shouted a challenge. Rockson frowned. No time for an elegant means of stopping them, not now. He felt foolish when he reached for his shotpistol and only found an empty holster. *Lost the damned thing somewhere!*

One of the swordsmen smiled a missing-toothed grin. "Do you think we would come to you with swords if you had a pistol? We saw it fall!"

So, there was only one recourse — the sword he carried. Rockson reached for the long, heavy Katama sword and pulled it from his scabbard as the samurai rushed forward with glistening swords raised over their heads.

The attackers' biceps and pectoral muscles rippled as they advanced toward the Doomsday Warrior, swinging their blades like twin scythes. Rockson darted to the left, away from the near miss of one steely blade, and tried to compose himself to raise the Katama into the proper position. He was *not* an expert at this, but Chen had taught him something of the noble art of swordsmanship in their many practice sessions in Century City's gymnasium. That lesson would be tested now!

"Let's see," Rockson said aloud, "that special grip is sorta like this — "

No time for any more rumination! They were upon him again, eager to take advantage of his momentary gathering of wits. They separated so they could come from *both* sides. Good! Chen had shown Rock what to do in that kind of situation. He employed the ancient technique of Master Uechi—hitting one opponent's sword with a quick thrust of your blade, joining its weight to your opponent's blade to meet the second man's thrust.

The method *did* stop the swords of the two samurai in midair, sending sparks of metal flying. Rock silently thanked the ancient master!

Then Rock spun, sweeping the gathering of three swords to the side—again, an Uechi move. With a sudden, blindingly fast motion, Rock pulled his sword out of the tangle and twisted his wrist, delivering a horizontal slash at torso height as he got in a crouched position. The shorter samurai was not prepared for the slash. Twisting ungainfully to the side, he was still caught in his thigh by the blade. He screamed out an anguished epithet and collapsed.

The larger samurai took advantage of his friend's demise to push Rockson down with a lightning dropkick. Rockson went down and rolled away, then saw the blade descend where he had just been and clank against the floor.

Rock grabbed the fallen samurai and used him as a shield to get back up. The body took the full sword blow of his frenetic companion. The mighty blow nearly split the samurai open from neck to pelvis, sending coagulating blood splashing. The big samurai drew back in horror.

Rockson grabbed the sliced man's Katama off the floor. He still had his own blade.

Now for the *double-dicer!* Swinging both swords at the remaining samurai, as if Rockson were a food processor chasing a carrot, the Doomsday Warrior advanced.

The samurai cut and ran—something a samurai should *never* do! Rock aimed and threw both swords, skewering the coward against a wooden display case containing a Tokyo diorama. The man jerked a few times and then hung limply, oozing red.

Rockson turned back to the elevator to continue his work, but cursed as he saw a KGBer lifting up the shoulder bag full of explosives. The Soviet started to run away with it. Perhaps the Russian didn't know what the pack contained, or perhaps he knew; but in any case, he was absconding with the package that meant life or death to the world!

The angry Freefighter tackled him. They fell atop the severed samurai, and Rockson and the Russian struggled with each other in a glop of blood and intestines. They grappled for the man's Tokarev pistol. The Soviet was a fiercely strong man and got his pistol up, bending it toward Rockson's chest despite Rock's best effort. But the American bit down on his hand until the fingers open, twisted the pistol at the man's face and squeezed the trigger. The man's anguished features exploded into bloody fragments.

The Doomsday Warrior rose, wiping blood out of his eyes, only to confront a tall blond KGBer carrying a smoking SMG. The man sneered and lifted the barrel at Rock. This time, however, Rock didn't have to do a thing to defend himself. The Russians turned as he heard the sudden approach of sandalled feet.

It was Morimoto, swishing his silvery sword in a figure eight. He screamed out a primitive challenge.

The Russian tried to fire but in a micro-second took the blow from the descending sword on his right forearm. The SMG clattered to the floor with the Red's right hand and wrist still attached. He hadn't *let go* of the weapon after all.

The next Katama blow came as the Red stood frozen, staring at the hoselike squirt of blood issuing from his half-arm. Morimoto's sword came directly at his pate, and the Russian made no move to counter. The razor-sharp instrument sliced his skull neatly in half, down to his collarbone. And he sank to the ground.

Morimoto tugged his ancentral blade away, then wiped it on the man's jacket. "Continue your work, friend."

The Doomsday Warrior nodded, grabbed the satchel of explosives and headed back to the elevator. The hell with the lock picking, he thought. Prying the dead Russian's SMG from the severed fingers, Rock fired the full clip into the elevator lock button.

Brute force accomplished the job. The silver elevator door opened. Rockson sighed, shouldered the explosive satchel, stepped into the silver car and pressed "72." The door shut out the cacophony of screams and shots in the building lobby, and Rock rode up in silence.

This was too easy — wasn't it? Rockson watched the floors rapidly click off. Sixty-one, sixty-two.

He looked casually around at the elevator car. Something was odd. What was different?

Yes! The little hand rail that had been at the back of the elevator—probably to prevent the wall being damaged by carts—had been neatly removed. The screw holes from the screws that had held the rail in place had been almost invisibly filled.

Why had the rail been removed?

Then Rockson understood that because the rail was missing there were perhaps only seconds to act—or he would die!

Quickly he reached to his belt and took out his balisong knife. He dug out the two highest buttons on the elevator panel, "73" and "Tower." The buttons popped out and rolled about the elevator's floor.

Rock sheathed the knife, and jammed the index fingers of both his hands into the holes he had made—the only holes he could *possibly* make in the steel-walled elevator.

The elevator's floor suddenly dropped out from under his feet! He watched the floor panel fall, hanging seventy-one floors above the basement, supported only by his two fingers.

CHAPTER 25

Detroit ejected a hot magazine from his Liberator and looked around. There were KGB bodies everywhere. The Americans and their allies now controlled the lobby, but the cost had been high. Ten samurai and two Polynesians had died in the fighting; he and McCaughlin were wounded. Detroit's wound was just a nick on his ankle, bandaged with a piece of KGB uniform, but feisty McCaughlin had a bullet lodged somewhere between his collarbone and his heart. Chen was looking after him. And there were still KGBers coming in around the building from the surrounding city.

Morimoto had explained that Rockson had entered the elevator and was probably already planting the bomb upstairs. Their job was to keep control until he came back down, then break out of the building before it was blown to shit.

Suddenly Detroit heard a clatter and hard thud in the elevator shaft. Fearing the worst, Detroit went to the elevator and used a twisted piece of metal to pry the door open. He was greeted by darkness and heavy dust. He snapped his flashlight on and swept its beam downward. The light revealed the shattered remains of the floor of the elevator—twisted tiles and bent metal.

"Rock?" Detroit said, "are you—alive?"

No answer. Scheransky came over and gasped out, "Do you think he's dead?"

Detroit said, "I'll find out." He climbed down and started to loosen the twisted wreckage. In a minute he shouted with relief. "Good news—I don't see a body. Rock must have grabbed on somewhere above. He'll need help!" But just then, there was a series of rapid fire shots from outside the tower lobby. Detroit shouted, "Keep the bastards at bay men; I'm going up the elevator shaft."

"I'm coming too," said Chen, rushing over. "Leilani is handling McCaughlin; he's not too bad off."

"ME TOO," Archer added, bounding over to the group gathered at the open elevator shaft.

Detroit said, "Rock said I'm in charge while he's upstairs. *I* decide who climbs. Archer, I don't trust the cable with your weight."

"MEEE CLIMB," Archer protested.

"Look," Detroit said with exasperation, "it's like this—only Chen will climb. I want to go up too, pal, but we're needed down here."

Chen nodded. "I'm best at this. I'll find out what gives." Detroit didn't want Archer to hear his next remarks to Chen, so he whispered them in the Chinese-American's ear: "If Rock's dead—or unable to finish the job—find the satchel of explosives and finish."

Chen nodded. He immediately started climbing up

214

the cable.

Seventy-one stories up, Rockson, hanging by his very *strong* fingers, heard the elevator door slide open. He was hanging to the right, out of sight of the KGB men who now peered into the floorless elevator car from Killov's domain.

"Ha—it worked, Stanislov," said the blond with the cheek scar, "We have rid ourselves of Rockson! I told you the elevator trap would work!"

"Yes, indeed," the older man replied. "Now let's get to the windows, keep the .105 in action. There might be more of the attackers coming in *behind* our reinforcements!"

The pair of Soviet officers left the elevator area. Rockson, with a painful, desperate try, swung his feet onto the landing as soon as they were gone. He was sure he had broken both fingers; but they weren't his only trigger fingers, and he could still use his fists if need be. A mutant could "put away" such pain—when he had to!

He walked through the ante-room of the suite like a cat—and again reached the doors of the room with the control panel. He nudged the door and, finding it open, pushed in. There were three men slumped at the lit-up panel.

"What the hell?"

Rockson felt each man's neck for a pulse, and just as he expected by the blood caked on their ears and around their lips, they were dead. Why?

His mutant instincts, the same feeling for danger

that had saved him in the elevator, now tickled him again. He had to do something. Rock looked around. There was a rack with—what the hell was it? Some sort of heavy earmuffs! Just one pair.

Rock picked it up. It was more like a plastic shield for the ears, the kind airport workers use around jets.

That clicked. The *sound* of the crystal weapon had killed these technicians. Rock quickly put the pair of super earmuffs on. A readout was flashing "OVER-RIDE." What did that mean? Maybe the panel was being bypassed. Killov must be somewhere, *directly* controling the ray weapon.

Rockson noted that the central seat was missing. He looked around—*nothing.* He looked up and saw a circular grey bulge in the ceiling of the room, directly over the missing control seat. Was Killov up there?

Rock decided that he must be! But it looked like hours' work to break in. There didn't seem to be any crack in the uniform grey convexity of the steel sanctuary above.

Rockson smiled. Okay, I *won't* go in! If Killov is in there—let him stay there and die when the bomb goes off!

Rockson went back toward the elevator shaft, determined to plant the seventy pounds of high explosives one flight up—alongside Killov's domain. He'd kill two birds with one stone—blow the crystal to bits along with its mad owner.

It took a lot of awkward, dangerous maneuvering for Rockson to get himself—and the seventy pounds of explosives—up through the elevator's trap door. Still, after ten minutes, he was standing on the car's roof and packing the *plastique* into a big lump. He jammed a radio-controlled blasting cap fuse into the mass of death, then made his way back down to the 71st floor and swung back into the carpeted anteroom.

As he did this, Rockson heard a grunting just yards below. Someone was coming up the cable.

Crouching down with his big blade at the ready, he saw *Chen* scramble into the room.

"God, it's you!" He put down the knife.

"Rock," Chen gasped breathlessly. "You're alive!" Chen quickly explained why he had made the climb.

Rock handed Chen the radio-control detonator. "Get back to the others. If I'm not back in ten minutes, get out of the building—and blow it up with this."

"Why aren't you coming down with me?"

Rock grimaced. "Because of Killov. He's here. I'm going to kill him personally. I just don't trust the bastard to die in the explosion! I've blown him up—or thought I did—several times in the last few years!"

Chen resisted leaving, but Rock made it an order.

Once Chen left the way he had come, Rockson piled furniture until he could climb up and touch the surface of the bulging grey metal in the ceiling. It was cold steel. There *was* a micro-thin seam—too narrow for a blade. Rock had to open it somehow if he wanted to personally waste the madman.

He pondered the problem of how to get in. It seemed insurmountable.

Killov, in his darkened domain, was lining up Baltimore as a target again. This time he wouldn't miss. Suddenly he heard a knock. Who could be knocking on his floor? He should ignore it, and yet, he was a curious man. Killov clicked on the intercom. "Who is it? Who dares—"

"Sir!" a hoarse voice yelled in Japanese-accented Russian. "It is Nakashima! I am alive! You buried my twin brother's body, not mine. I am *alive*, master. Let me in."

Killov nearly fainted with relief. Yes! Of course! It was too *tragic* to be true! Nakashima wasn't dead; his dear friend had returned to him, to share his glory.

"Oh my friend, come in, come in!" Killov shouted. "I'm dilating the door!"

Rockson saw the micro-slit in the grey metal globe start bending. Slowly, like a lens shutter, a hole was appearing. No time to waste! The Doomsday Warrior dove into the aperture, just as it was wide enough to take him in, and started to pull himself up.

The tall, very gaunt man in a tight black outfit gasped out, *"You,"* and reached for a switch. The door hole snapped shut on Rockson's body. He was jammed waist high, halfway in, halfway out of the strange dark chamber filled with stars.

218

Rock winced in pain, trying to pull himself first in, then out. Nothing worked. He was immobilized.

His eyes adjusted to the near-total darkness, and Rockson beheld Killov, the Skull, standing over him.

Mad laughter erupted. Killov's neck veins pulsed in sadistic excitement when he saw that the Doomsday Warrior was pinned. "Well—you *surprised* and *disappointed* me, Rockson. You are very clever to imitate Nakashima . . . but not clever enough. I wish I could draw out this moment more . . . savor it. You look a fine sight. This is an ingnominious end for the fabulous Doomsday Warrior, wouldn't you say?"

Killov lifted a shiny automatic pistol in his left hand.

"Fuck you, asshole," Rock said, expecting a bullet.

"My, my. Is cursing the last thing you wish to do in this life?" That mad laugh again. Then Killov, instead of squeezing off a round, put the automatic down. The colonel lifted his right arm. It seemed to Rockson to be peculiarly thicker than his left one.

"I will make you suffer, Rockson! A bullet is too easy, despite my eagerness to get back to my ultimate weapon. This arm's sleeve contains a firing mechanism for a compressed air gun. It can fire several very long spikes. And they are tipped with a poison that will give agonizing pain for sixty seconds—then death!"

Killov pulled back his sleeve, and Rockson saw a glint of sharp metal. Then Killov let loose a barrage of steel spikes. The shafts dug deep into Rock's shoulder—but not his chest—because he twisted suddenly. Still, Rock was seized with immense pain. He groaned as the pain coursed from the poisoned wounds in his body. Then the pain grew and grew.

He screamed out several times in agony. After a minute, he jerked spasmodically, and then his eyes rolled up and he slumped over.

Killov stepped over to Rockson and kicked him in the face. *No response,* even though the trapped man's nose broke with a crunch.

"So, now you are finally dead, and *I* rule the world," Killov intoned.

The colonel turned, retook his control seat and started fiddling with the dials.

Rockson lifted his head an inch. All of the death-jerks hid his hands working up along his body. Now he had room to silently pull himself out of the darkened chamber. Rockson, controlling the torturous pain wracking his body, blood oozing from his boot-snapped nose, lept down onto the carpet below Killov's lair. He dove into the elevator shaft and started sliding down the cable. In just seconds Chen would set off the explosives!

CHAPTER 26

Killov, who had returned to his seat sure Rockson was dead, was set to destroy Baltimore. Then the situation screen lit up. Several lines of green lights were depicted coming up at his space mirror from the Soviet Union. All the lines were missiles, the readout said, and were tipped with nuclear warheads!

"No!" Killov gasped, "no, please . . ." He didn't know exactly who to address his earnest prayer to. Sometimes the colonel sensed that he was serving a *darkness* beyond the stars. To that dark force he directed his cry. "Please, Dark One, don't let them destroy my weapon!"

Suddenly the green lines stopped dead, hundreds of miles below the space mirror, and slowly winked out.

Killov smiled; he remembered the manuals told that the space mirror system had its own defenses. The defenses were over a hundred years old—then again, there is no atmosphere to damage delicate parts in space. He dismissed the mystical element in what happened. Systems had powered up and acted, that was all.

He snapped on his worldwide radio connection, beaming his hideously enlarged, echoing voice throughout the planet on all frequencies. "Attention. This is Killov. I have allowed you all a little more time in order for you to see the failure of the missile attack on my space mirror. Now you all know my power is unstoppable. Surrender at once; *that is all!*"

Killov put the headset on and listened to a frantic set of surrender offers coming from Russia, from China, and even from President Zhabnov in the U.S.S.A.

"One at a time, one at a time," he snapped. "I want only one man to answer me—and that is Premier Vassily himself. Vassily? Are you there?"

"Yes, you bastard" came a dry unsteady voice. The grandfather of the world was on the line! The voice that Killov knew so intimately well, his old boss Vassily, ruler of the World Soviet, said, "I surrender, Killov! Come and take your prize—come take Moscow. I am old and tired . . . and *you win.*"

Killov's eyes narrowed in suspicion. "You are not just stalling for time? Planning another counterattack?"

"No, we surrender. We have seen you destroy so much that we conclude your power is absolute. To save the world, I surrender it. The World Soviet States are *all yours!*"

Though such a surrender was inevitable, Killov still had somehow not really *expected* it. He had longed for Vassily *not* to reply, so he could broil the capital

222

city of the world—Moscow—to ashes.

The colonel hesitated. What should he do? Accept surrender? Or laugh in their faces and keep destroying targets?

Killov, after a long minute, said, "Okay, I'll send my representative to Moscow—to assume power until I arrive. In the meantime, Vassily, I must now eradicate the American rebels in their Century City. I will *not* tolerate the American resistance like you have, Vassily. My rule shall be absolute!"

"Killov," the premier's aged voice cracked out. "Don't! They will call you and surrender, I am sure. It must be some technical problem that has prevented the Americans from replying to you!"

"Too late for surrender calls," Killov said. "They will all die." Forgetting Baltimore, Killov started redirecting the space mirror toward the western United States.

The Freefighter force ran in a hail of tracer bullets through a screen of heavy smoke. Dodging around an arriving tank, they reached a department store's shattered display windows. *"In,* we go in the windows," the black Freefighter yelled, jumping up and smashing the last shards of broken glass to clear the way. He was followed in by Chen, who together with Archer helped lift a limping Ted Rockson into the display. Rockson had managed to defeat the poison that the spikes had unleashed in him—his mutant constitution—and had reached the lobby. There, he was greeted by the others. Chen had disobeyed orders;

their leader was two minutes past the deadline. Then they all broke out of the closing steel ring of KGB reinforcements.

"Rock, how soon do we explode the bomb?" Detroit asked.

"Now," Rock said. "Everyone—get behind something—Takashimaya Department Store's walls look thick."

"By Lenin," Scheransky uttered. "I sure hope they *are*—"

His words were cut off when Chen pressed the button of the remote detonator. The Earth shook; the blast nearly threw them off their feet. Rockson peered from behind a thick support pillar and saw the tower was coming down in two sections. Spinning down, separately, end over end, like some gigantic stunt driver, was the crystal.

Rockson and the others watched the KGBers in the plaza try to get out of the way of a million tons of twisted steel girders and fractured masonry—and fail. Then, as smaller debris peppered their sanctuary, they retreated farther into the darkened department store.

Chen said, "We did it Rock! No one could have survived that! Certainly Killov is dead!"

CHAPTER 27

When the heavy dust clouds cleared sufficiently, the victorious Americans and their allies left their shelter. They walked toward a strange glow in the mists. Rockson had an idea of what the flickering glow was, but it was Scheransky, leading the group, who cried out: "God it didn't break. The crystal is *intact*. How can this be?"

Rock had no answer. He stood up on a pile of debris to get a clear view. The huge crystal was half embedded in the broken pavement of the intersection. It still pulsed with blue and green energy.

Scheransky touched Rockson's shoulder and said, "It is like the thing is alive, like it has a heartbeat — only colors, not pulses."

"It *is* a living being," said Leilani. She shucked her flak jacket and stepped past them, bending to touch its shimmering surface. She was immediately suffused in the crystal's glow, which turned a pale blue as it engulfed her. Leilani put her ear to the twelve-foot, circular crystal and listened for a while to something nobody else could hear, stroking the thing like a baby.

Then she started sobbing.

"What is it?" Rock asked. "What do you hear?"

Leilani turned and said, "Oh Rockson, it is so sorry for what it has been forced to do! The Gnaa crystal wants to die, but cannot. It doesn't want to live with the memory of all the destruction. It says it is not damaged. Only heat can destroy it. Heat of many thousands of degrees. It wants us to help it die!"

"Let's get out of here," implored Scheransky. "We did the job. The tower's gone, Killov's gone, and—"

"No," Rockson said, as he turned. "Whether or not Leilani's right about the crystal having a soul, she is right about one thing. The crystal has to be destroyed! It's the most dangerous thing in the world. We've got to melt it down."

"Maybe," suggested Chen, "we can set it on fire with gasoline."

"No," Rockson said. "I believe Leilani's right. It needs more heat than that to destroy it."

"The only way," sobbed Leilani, "is to immerse it in Mount Fuji's volcanic heat. That is how it wants to die. We must throw it into Mount Fuji's crater!"

"Why that's *ridiculous,"* Detroit protested, keeping his eyes peeled for enemy soldiers. "To drag it there would take hours—if we could even do it at all."

Rockson had to admit the request seemed unfulfillable. There was a sudden noise. It sounded like air hissing out of a tube. Rock spun around. Everywhere, he saw people pouring out from hiding places in wrecked buildings and heading toward them. The surviving citizens of the city.

Morimoto shouted at them in Japanese, telling

hem the party around the crystal was friends, not
ussians.

The Freefighters stood and watched as the giant
rowd surged forward. Leilani stood there in her
arong, suffused with blue light in the aura that
ulsed out of the Gnaa. The crowd was surging closer,
houting and pointing at Leilani and the strange
rystal.

The foremost of the crowd fell to make prostrations
n the street, as if they were worshiping. The
thers followed suit. It grew very silent, like a re-
gious event.

Still suffused with blue light, Leilani raised one
and and said softly but clearly, "Know this, that I
m the Gnaa, a creation of mankind, yet I am the
irst intelligent creation. I apologize for what I have
one and only wish to end my existence before more
vil men arise to use me once more. Please—take me
o Mount Fuji volcano and put me in its cleansing
ire."

Rock's jaw opened wide. Leilani had a transfixed
xpression; her eyes were empty. She was speaking not
or herself, but at the direction of the crystal, in some
ort of *link* with it again.

She lowered her head and stepped from the crystal;
he aura parted from her and faded. Rock put the
acket she had dropped back over her bare shoulders.
eilani smiled up at him. "It spoke?"

"Yes it spoke, through you," he said, holding her
hivering cold body close to him.

Leaders in the crowd now started to cry out direc-
ions, and many moved into the buildings again. They

returned quickly with lengths of cable and long heavy ropes.

Rock's troops looked at him blankly, with a what-do-we-do-now expression.

Rockson said, "What the hell, let's *do it!* Help attach the ropes to the crystal. Run them over to some of those trucks over by the department store. We'll see if we can drag the crystal up Mount Fuji."

Archer said, "GOOOD—MEE DRAGG BY SELF!" He jumped down next to the crystal and started to attach the first big cable around the girth of the thing. Rockson had been watching the mountain man as the crystal "talked" through Leilani. The look in the giant's eyes had told it all—he really empathized with the Gnaa. Perhaps it was because Archer was five percent crystal himself!

Rockson, as the others came to help Archer attach more cables to the crystal, scanned the tumble of smoldering wreckage scattered all about the square. Here and there he saw a jutting hand or foot—bodies buried in the jumble.

Was Killov really dead? He *must* be. All that remained of the tower were a few vertical girders at each of its four legs. And yet, the Doomsday Warrior felt no triumph.

"Hey Rock," Detroit called, "can you help me with this?" Rockson sighed and moved to help Detroit. McCaughlin, who had received a clean wound—a bullet had passed right through his shoulder—kept a watchful guard with an SMG as the Freefighters all pitched in.

Soon a dozen cables were wound around the Gnaa

ystal. Its glow could barely be seen, to entwined was s faceted bulk. They ran the cables over the trucks d attached them.

Rockson had worried that the operation would be iped at, but evidently if there were any KGB left, ey had gone to ground.

Unseen by Rockson and his men, a sinewy trembling hand jabbed out of the debris one hundred ards away, clawing for light and air. Another hand opped up, like a sprouting weed. Then the hands craped and pushed, until a bleeding thin-lipped nouth was uncovered.

The mouth spat out dirt and broken teeth and ucked in air.

Killov yet lived!

CHAPTER 28

With Morimoto and his men shouting instruction
ildly, the crowd of Japanese civilians was mobilized.
he crystal slowly was dislodged from its impact hole
y the combined pull of six trucks on the cable.

The broad avenue leading toward New Mount Fuji
as cleared of cars meanwhile. Rockson entered the
lack semi on the right side of the broad well-paved
reet and used the CB to shout out instructions to the
ther truckers: Chen, Detroit, Murf, Scheransky and
orimoto.

"Okay, let's keep it *even*. Keep alongside each other.
asy does it—five miles per hour!"

No one knew just how much the crystal weighed—
aybe ten tons—but it was heavy. They had their
ccelerators halfway down, and the truck wheels
arted to slip and smoke; but it started to move.

To the immense cheering of the crowds lining the
ay and waving at the drivers, they headed toward the
olcano's slope, five miles away. It was then another
ve miles, Rock knew, up to the summit's wide crater.
e didn't have *any* idea how they were going to

231

manage the ascent to the top at all. But putting firs
things first, Rock decided he'd get to the slope, an
then figure it out.

Rock hoped the cables would hold, and that th
KGB that were left in the city would keep in th
woodwork like the roaches they were. Without Killo
to rally them, they might *never* reappear. Yet som
instinct told Rock the battle was *not* over.

It took two hours, but the trucks finally pulled th
crystal to the end of the avenue. Ahead, the roa
became a steeply ascending, winding narrow road,
pilgrims' path, leading to the sacred volcano's crate
10,000 feet up. Rockson, put his truck in neutra
using the CB to tell the other drivers to do the sam

He slammed on the handbrake and opened th
door, stepping out. He stood scratching his head
looking into the mists above. *No way* was this bab
going to get the hell up there!

Leilani, who had been following the crystal at th
head of a huge crowd, now came up to Rockson. Sh
touched his sleeve. He turned and started to smile
Then Rock saw that her countenance again wore
strange empty expression. The look in her dark eye
was far away. Leilani's voice was soft and melodiou
again as she spoke: "I, the crystal, have a way to . .
the summit. Detach the cables, except the one to you
truck, Rockson. Start pulling again; I will transmi
my power to the truck."

"Leilani?" Rock asked, moving his right hand bacl
and forth in front of her face. She just stared straigh
ahead, unseeing.

"I will come with you. . . ." Leilani intoned. Sh

started around the semi's cab and got in the shotgun seat.

"Okay . . ." Rock said to no one in particular, "I guess I will just play it that way!"

He ordered his men to detach four of the pull cables from the crystal, then got back in the driver's seat. He took one quick look over at Leilani. Her eyes fluttered; she turned, smiled at him and said, "How did I get in here?"

"I'll explain later; we have to take a little ride."

Before he could touch the gears, the truck shifted into first and revved forward powerfully without his foot touching the accelerator. The handle of the twelve-gear shift suffused with a dull blue glow and started to move itself. The truck began to climb at about fifteen miles per hour, pulling the crystal with ease. How the hell the wheels didn't spin out under it, Rockson couldn't imagine. Maybe the crystal was putting pressure *down* on the truck too, to keep it from skidding.

Rockson steered for all he was worth as the truck tore ahead. Twenty, thirty, forty miles per hour it gained speed, screeching around each hairpin curve. Through the rearview mirror Rock could see the crystal whipping around the curves at the end of its tether behind him. And way down the slope, moving much more slowly, the other trucks followed.

In no time at all, they had made the steep climb and screeched to an engine-steaming halt at the very edge of the crater.

They were parked so close to the precipitous drop to the bubbling lava pool at the bottom of the crater that Rock and Leilani had to get out her side.

Leilani had that glazed-eyed look again. "This is the best way — I wish to die. Please push me over the edge — both of you."

Rockson, feeling *very* eerie, unhitched the cable. With Leilani assisting, once she came out of her trance, they put their combined shoulders to the crystal. It was ridiculous to think they could move an object that could bend in the pavement of the parking area, *but they did*.

Slowly, they edged it to the lip of the crater and poised it there. With tears in her eyes, Leilani pushed. Then she stepped back and watched the crystal slowly lean over the edge and fall. It *slid* for a while down a pumice incline, then started tumbling, gathering speed, then bouncing, like a ball. It was heading directly for the molten pool of red hot lava cradled in the center of the volcanic crater.

The crystal glowed red, white and blue alternately. Bounding once more, it fell into the red molten pool, splashing lava a hundred feet into the air. Sparkling and sizzling, the crystal slowly sank, sending lightning bolts streaking into the clouded heavens.

The other trucks pulled in beside Rockson's now, and the drivers jumped out. The backs of the trucks were filled with citizens. All came hesitantly to the crater's edge to watch the bubbling magma of the volcano slowly take in the crystal.

"Well," Rockson started to say, "it's over—"

There was a dull thud-thud-thud in the air. "A

234

chopper!" Detroit yelled. "Coming in from the west!"

Rock sighted a sleek, black wasp-shaped military helicopter heading directly at the gathering. It was coming in low and was armed with racks of rockets slung under its stubby wings. It—looked familiar!

"*Killov's* chopper," Rock gasped, recognizing the silhouette against the blue sky. "He's alive! Everyone direct fire at the chopper!"

The Freefighters set their Liberator SMGs on full automatic. They could see the tracer shells hit the heli—to no effect.

"It's heavily armored," Chen lamented. "We can't—" He didn't finish his words, for a set of six rockets was fired at them in a spread pattern. Rock knew they had mere seconds to live.

"Quickly," he shouted, "get into the crater. There's a steep slope before it drops off vertically. Hang on as best you can."

Not everyone managed to get over the lip. The rockets hit, shaking the ground, sending up plumes of metal fragments and flame. Those that had made it in slid down the loose pumice, clawing for a hold.

Several Japanese citizens and one Surfcomber—Knudson—got caught in the explosions. Knudson tumbled into the crater, his body aflame. He tumbled past Rockson's desperate grasp and over the edge of the drop, then fell screaming into the lava. There was a hiss as he hit the 5000-degree molten pool.

Archer had caught a bit of the blasts and his coat of fur was afire. He rolled over and over to put the flames out successfully.

The chopper meanwhile zoomed over their heads

235

and started to turn back for another shot.

"What do we do now?" Chen, who had landed next to Rock asked.

"Maybe — pray."

Suddenly Archer shouted out. It was more like a battle roar. The man had thrown off his half-burned bearskin and had reached into his quiver. He extracted a harpoonlike home-made arrow and notched it into his bowstring. Pulled back by the heavy musculature of the giant near-mute's arm, the immense arrow turned upward. Archer bent the titanium alloy bow to its maximum, so that the metal string sang when its unbelievable power was unleashed and the arrow let fly. Whistling, it soared upward like a missile and hit the tail rotor of the deadly sky machine. The tail rotor shattered and the craft spun out of control, trailing smoke.

As everyone cheered, the heli barely cleared the far volcano rim and disappeared from sight.

"*That's* what we do," Rock said, standing up and brushing himself off.

"Is Killov really dead now?" Leilani asked.

"I doubt it. He has more lives than a cat!" They all scrambled up the pumice slope and back onto the pavement.

And just in time, for the earth trembled beneath them. In the crater, the lava pit erupted violently. It was a powerful blast, like a giant molten hot *burp*. A geyser of steam and fiery magma shot up over the crater, threatening to rain down on them.

"Everyone off the volcano," Rock shouted, but they needed no encouragement. As small steaming rocks

236

fell all around, the crowd surged back down the slope.

Rock called out to his men. "Freefighters! Follow me! We circle the rim and go get Killov. Slap some more mags in your Liberators, and let's finish the bastard off. *For Knudson!*"

CHAPTER 29

Killov, his face blackened by flame, his uniform in tatters, staggered from the badly damaged heli, assisted by the pilot, Major Smerdskov. The gunner, his teeth smashed in, blood oozing from his lips, also managed to get out. Then the craft blew up. Killov sat down on a slag rock. The colonel was at a loss as to what to do or where to go.

Only these two men were left from his entire 500-man KGB death-force! They had three machine pistols and a few rounds of ammo. That was all that stood between Killov and the awesome vengeance of the Doomsday Warrior.

But Killov's face animated with determination; his black eyes flickered with passionate resolve. He hadn't hidden for two years like a night-rat in the Moscow Library eating the chewing gum readers had stuck under the tables, devouring crusts of sandwiches left behind, *to die now!* He hadn't plumbed the alleyways in the slums of that immense Imperial city searching for and gathering desperate men to join him, *only to die now!* He hadn't journeyed the steppes of Siberia in the dead of winter, crossed the world's largest ocean and suffered so much, *to accept defeat now!*

"Never," he shouted. *"Never* will I be defeated! We go into the crater," Killov said. "There are no doubt many natural passages—old lava tunnels—that we can hide in—"

"But," Smerdskov protested, "we can't go into an active volcano. What if—what if the tunnels we seek suddenly fill with lava? Or steam?"

Killov's small eyes narrowed, "No guts eh? How about you, Derminkovsky?"

The gunner, who had been dabbing at his teeth with a torn piece of his shirt, looked at Killov standing there. All the officers had known that Killov was rowing with one oar out of the water, but what he now proposed was not perverted or violent—it was sheer *madness.* Derminkovsky decided he would shoot Killov—and maybe Smerdskov too, when he got the chance. Then he'd strip off his uniform and try to get lost in the island's population. Derminkovsky thought it was the best idea he'd ever had! He was swarthy, and his eyes were rather almond shaped—like his Ukranian grandmother's eyes. He could pull it off! But it was best to play along—for now.

He shrugged. "We might as well try the volcano, Colonel. Or our enemies will surely be here any minute."

"Thank you," Killov said, "for your confidence." Killov pulled his pistol, spun and shot Smerdskov point-blank in the face. The man slumped to the dirt, spraying blood from the hole where his nose had been. "Let's go," Killov said. "We don't need a *quitter!*"

Killov made Derminkovsky go first into the crater. The man might be okay, he thought, but then again, he could be faking allegiance. They ran downward at an angle, descending rapidly, slipping on pieces of slag and the sandy pumice. Before them, thousands of feet down, the lava bubbled and steamed. You could feel its heat on the winds.

A hundred yards along, they were suddenly knocked from their feet by a violent tremor. They slid more than fifty feet farther through the steam and flames, almost fell over the precipice, before they could arrest their descent.

"Onward," Killov yelled, waving his pistol at the gunner who was wild-eyed in fear now. "Just keep going. *That way!*"

Killov was nearly exhausted when he saw a bump in the dark soot about a hundred yards ahead. "There, Derminkovsky! I think that might be what we're looking for. We head in that direction. It's got to be a fissure—or a tunnel!"

Indeed, they came to a dark opening, circular, nearly high enough for a man to stand upright in. "Well, what are you waiting for! Get in there!" Killov snarled. He wanted the gunner in front of him to serve as a guinea pig. There might be deadly odorless gasses in the dark tunnel. Or there could be a sudden drop-off.

In a few moments they were both groping in the

darkness. The gunner tried to go slow, but Killov stuck his machine pistol into Derminkovsky's back. "Keep moving," he insisted. They continued along, winding slowly through the sinuous tunnel until they saw a dim red flickering light ahead. The air was heavy and sulphurous, and there was a low roar, like steam issuing from a pipe.

"My God," yelled Derminkovsky, stopping in his tracks. "I won't go any farther. There must be molten lava close ahead!"

Killov stepped back and pulled up his left sleeve. He didn't want to fire his machine pistol in the tunnel. It could send the whole mountain down upon him. But he'd had enough of quitters! Killov fired twin steel spikes tipped with poison into the coward's back.

Screaming in pain, Derminkovsky slammed to the tunnel floor. Killov stepped over his twitching body and continued walking down the pipelike tunnel.

It grew brighter and brighter ahead as he walked. The rational part of his mind told Killov he was walking to his doom, but Killov had a wild hunch that he should go on. Or maybe it *wasn't* a hunch after all. There was *something* about that noise, and that red glow . . . that *beckoned!*

CHAPTER 30

The Doomsday Warrior and his squad came upon the wrecked helicopter and found the body of one uniformed man. Rock bent over the man and observed the wide, bloody face. "Not Killov!"

"Look," Chen said. "Footprints!"

They followed the set of bootprints away from the wreck, until they came to the lip of the crater. Rockson took his binocs out and scanned the vast pit below. Yes, Killov and a companion had fled into the crater itself. He could see their long sliding boot steps continuing for hundreds of yards downward. And then there was a long solid trail, as if the two men had slid out of control—probably when the tremor had struck. The slide marks ended at the vertical drop-off. It was obvious that Killov and the other man had run like fools to their doom.

Rock put down the binocs and said, "You can put your shotpistols back into your holsters. They're goners. Let's get the hell out of here; I don't like the way that lava pit is bubbling and rising. I think the volcano might—"

Before Rockson could finish his words, a titanic geyser of molten lava and hot steam—more voluminous than the last eruption—shot from the central lava lake. The mountain shook anew.

"Run for it. The whole shebang is gonna blow," he shouted. "Get to the boats!"

Running down the slope, they could see the *Surf City* and the *Dragon* sailing into dockside at the city pier. It was a wonderful sight!

They made good time running down the volcano and were glad to find some vehicles scattered about in the street. Many had been abandoned with the keys in them, either during the fighting or when the tower collapsed. Rock got one old Mazda van started, and the team piled in. They drove madly toward the docks, on sidewalks when the streets were blocked.

When they arrived at the waterfront, people were already pouring onto the pair of sailing ships. The ships were over-filled with frightened islanders and threatening to capsize.

The citizens had good reason to be frightened; but this had to be stopped, or they'd all perish, Rock realized.

Rockson screeched to a halt and jumped out of the truck. He turned to see towering plumes of black smoke erupting upward out of the volcano. Red rivulets of lava slid down the mountain. The roar of the explosion washed over the dock area.

"This isn't gonna work," Rock yelled. "Two vessels can't evacuate the whole island. We have to get some of the people *off!*" Then Rockson saw, out at sea, heading their way, a vast fleet of junks. "The fisherman and his friends are coming! That will help."

He saw his Bushido leader friend wave in his direction from a piling and pushed through a scramble of bodies to reach him. "Morimoto," Rock shouted into his ear, "you have got to tell them in Japanese that only women and children get on these ships. More ships are coming."

He pointed to the sea. Morimoto nodded. "When they see the extra ships, it will calm them. We have found some KGB megaphones. I will try to organize the evacuation."

The ground shook repeatedly, and rising waves started tossing the docked ships. Morimoto and several other swordsmen started haranguing the masses over the confiscated loudspeakers. In a matter of a few minutes, some order was created. The men on the sail ships got back ashore, while the women and children were placed aboard and sailed off on the two ships. The crews headed the craft for the coral atolls ten miles distant. They would quickly disembark the refugees and then come back for more passengers, Morimoto told Rockson. In the meantime, the first of the many fishing vessels entered the harbor to the sound of wild cheering.

The Freefighters and their allies directed the orderly loading of the fishing boats. These sturdy vessels, too, were filled and started off through the choppy seas. Rock worried about time; they needed more time. Behind, at the edge of the city, houses were starting to catch fire as the lava rivers reached them.

Detroit, coming up alongside Rockson, said, "It looks like this is the end of New Tokyo."

Rock said grimly, "Yes. I hope the docks last until the ships return."

The streets nearest the docks were afire with running streams of lava by the time Rock and his Freefighters jumped aboard the last crowded fishing boat. No one had been left behind—at least they hoped so.

The small creaking junk raised its broad sail and made rapid speed away from the holocaust on rising winds, as the sun was blotted out by thick smoke.

Within ten minutes their craft neared the coral islands. Rock was concerned about two things now: He had lost track of Leilani, and also, would the volcano send its deadly gasses in the safety isle's direction?

He waded ashore with the other man. Rock looked back at New Tokyo Island as the fiery spectacle unfolded. Geysers of red lava and plumes of mushrooming orange flame thousands of feet high were coming up now all over New Tokyo. The volcano had obviously opened up the fissures lacing the island. The sky filled with lightning, and it grew dark, though it was nowhere near sunset.

Rockson ran up and down the beach, shouting, "Leilani! Leilani!" Soon he despaired. Was she somehow left behind? Could it be that she was lost to him?

But the lovely island girl found Rockson, threw herself into his arms and said, "Oh — I thought you — oh, thank the gods you are safe." She kissed him passionately. They turned and watched the volcano blow its entire 10,000-foot head off. Red plumes spread like a giant Fourth of July explosion a mile out to sea, obliterating the island and its proud city in one second. A thunderous roar shook the atoll's sands.

Leilani asked, "Are we far enough away?"

Rock replied softly, "Yes. See, the wind is blowing the smoke *away* from us."

The populace lit torches and went down on their knees on the long, red sand beach, weeping and wailing.

"They have no home now," Leilani said sadly. Then she brightened up. "There is *lots* of room on Rarapani and its nearby islands. And much fresh water and breadfruit — and good land. We will take them there. My people will welcome them!"

Rock and the island princess stood watching the awesome spectacle of destruction unfold, arm in arm. After a while, Leilani turned to the Doomsday Warrior and said, "The Gnaa crystal is gone forever, Rockson. So I am no longer its servant. So I no longer have to be — *virgin*."

Rockson smiled, swept her up in his arms and carried her off toward a secluded palm grove.

Epilogue

Killov picked himself up off the cold metal floor of the strange chamber he had found inside the tunnel. In the diffuse light that seemed to come from everywhere or nowhere, he patted his uniform in place, adjusted and buttoned the askew collar and took stock of the situation:

He was in one piece. That was something he hadn't counted on when the volcanic explosion had knocked his feet from under him! He tried to remember the exact sequence of events leading up to this point. . . . He remembered his entering the metal room, a sliding door shutting suddenly behind him. . . . He remembered pounding on the door, shouting for release until—a force hit him!

Yes—he had been hit by something—and he had been pinned to the metal floor like a bug under a paperweight for a *long time*.

What the hell had happened?

He gingerly took a step. That's *odd* . . . his foot didn't reach the floor when he put it down again. Instead, the ceiling floated down at him, at an angle.

Frantically, he reached out to grab air. The room tumbled slowly now, and he realized he was floating in the air like a feather.

He tried to right himself, but every panicky motion of his arms or legs sent him twirling in the opposite direction.

No gravity.

Now he saw the source of the diffuse light: a round window. He was drifting toward it, and so he stopped fighting the movement. He floated slowly past the—porthole. That's what it was!

Outside, a globe of blue and white—the *Earth*.

He knew it wasn't just a projection. He was in weightless space. The volcano's room must have been inside a space craft. That explained being pinned down. The thing had taken off, the pinning-down was the acceleration.

He moaned in fear. No human being, as far as he knew, had been above the atmosphere since the space age ended with the nuclear war, over a hundred years ago.

Whose spaceship was it?

He did not wait long for the answer to his question, for the metal door slid open again, and he beheld a tall lean shape with a large bulbous head. It was immersed in shadow; he couldn't quite make out—

"Greetings," the shape said. "Welcome aboard the *Talon*."

"W-who—are you?" Killov stuttered.

The shape took a step forward into the light, and Killov screamed in fear and tried to get away. But he merely tumbled in the air, bouncing off a wall.

The thing that had spoken had the body of a man—but it had a rounded fish head and finned hands and feet.

Killov remembered the native superstition about a walking fish that devoured people. It was *true!*

The colonel resigned himself to the *end.* He tumbled uncontrollably closer to the thing until it reached out its webbed hands and snagged him. Killov stared into a pair of glassine eyes.

The walking fish held on to Killov with one hand and pulled its own head *off* with the other.

Inside the head—obviously a helmet, Killov now realized—there was a very ordinary face. A man with a bald pate and a thin brown moustache. He had puffy dark bags under his eyes, like he was not well.

"Perhaps you would like a pair of magnetic shoes?" the man offered. "And then we can talk of why I brought you here. You owe us your life, you know. And we mean to make you pay for your deliverance!"

Killov thought of striking out at the man until he saw the others who had come in the door. They had some sort of guns in their web-fingered gloves, and the barrels of those weapons were all pointed his way.

"We—can talk about what you—want from me," Killov said. "I—I'm sure *some* sort of arrangement can be made."